When The Day Dawned

When The Day Dawned

A Collection of Short Stories

SOM NATH ZUTSHI

TRANSLATED BY SHAFI SHAUQ

Vitasta

Published by
Renu Kaul Verma
Vitasta Publishing Pvt Ltd
4348/4C, Ansari Road, Daryaganj
New Delhi - 110 002
info@vitastapublishing.com

ISBN: 978-81-19670-66-6

First Edition 2024
MRP ₹495

First published in Kashmiri language in 1998

These short stories are entirely a work of fiction. Names, characters, events and incidents are entirely imaginary. Reference to real places, actual regions, institutions or community practices has been made in a fictitious manner. Any resemblance to actual persons, living or dead or actual events is purely coincidental.

Edited by Renu Arya
Cover Design by Rohit Gautam
Printed and bound at Thomson Press (India) Ltd, Faridabad.

This book is dedicated
to the characters our dear father gave life to
in his short stories.

(Late) Ashok Zutshi, Son
(He would be smiling from heaven)
Nalini Hakhu, Daughter
Veena Kaul, Daughter
Kalpana Kaul, Daughter
Abhinav Zutshi, Son

Contents

Preface

I feel great pleasure in bringing out the English version of the Sahitya Akademi Award winning short stories of my father-in-law, late Som Nath Zutshi.

As all his friends and acquaintances know, Mr Zutshi's roots were humble, having taken birth into a simple family. Keen in studies from his childhood and a very bright student, his passion was literature and at a very tender age he read some of the top authors of the world. As such, it was natural for him to step into the world of writing at the age of fifteen.

What followed was the history he made in the world of Kashmiri literature with contributions in several genres like short stories (the first written by anyone in Kashmiri language in 1948), dramas, and radio & TV plays. He translated the works of some of the world's most famous authors including Franz Kafka, Nikolai Gogol, Henrik Ibsen, besides many scientific journals. For his contribution, he received several honours and accolades in his lifetime as well as after. He wrote honestly, diligently and passionately from his heart.

Starting at an early age, he became a trendsetter in the field of Kashmiri literature and was a part of the grand exercise of creating platforms that he also headed, along with other stalwarts for young writers. This eventually became a base for writers in Kashmiri language.

His forte was not just writing stories, plays and dramas, but also acting in them and lending his voice to the radio plays.

The stories in this volume are experiences of any next door neighbor, or of common people like you, me and him. The emotions are deeply rooted in the heart and feelings expressed in the beautiful language. Simplicity of thought grips the mind because it is every one's thought who experiences life so intimately. The stories take your soul to the scene as if you are present in those situations. Even though the settings are local but the vision encompasses a world far beyond where it merges with the global reality of mankind that his sensitive mind grasped well.

Every word he wrote was a piece of joy as it came from his soul. The characters, situations, and background were from the places and the people around him that he loved the most. He never sought fame, but the masterpieces he produced spoke the truth and carried profound messages. Honours, accolades and achievements just followed.

We are extremely grateful to Prof Shafi Shauq who, in spite of his busy schedule, agreed to translate the book into English and also write an analytical introduction to the stories. Prof Shauq has already expressed his admiration for Zutshi Sahab's art in his books, especially in, *Kaeshir zabaan ti adibuk taveeryiekh* (A history of Kashmiri Language and Literature).

We are also grateful to Prof Neerja Mattoo, the reputed author and translator, who has also translated several of Mr Zutshi's stories that appeared in various books and journals including *The Greatest Kashmiri Stories Ever Told,* to write a Foreword to Mr Zutshi's works in Kashmiri language.

—Ramesh Kaul

Foreword

I am very happy that a collection of Som Nath Zutshi's Kashmiri short stories has been brought out in English. Now, non-Kashmiri speaking people can also be acquainted with this great short story writer, a major talent in fiction from Kashmir.

Storytelling has been a part of humanity from the beginning of time either to amuse themselves, or to find lessons from life; some incident or the other is enough to weave a plot and tell a story. Kashmir is no exception to this rule. It has also been a cradle of storytelling since ancient times. But the modern genre of short stories came very late to Kashmir. It was around 1948 that the first Kashmiri short story by Som Nath Zutshi, titled *'Yeli phol gash'* (When the Light Dawned) was written. It was published in a Kashmiri Journal, *'Kong Posh'* which had just been started after the fall of the autocratic rule of the Maharaja. Freedom was in the air and aspirations were high. Many of the thinkers and writers of that time were deeply influenced by the changing times. They had a revolutionary fervour on their minds and wanted to serve as the conscience of the people through their stories. Their purpose was to transform society, to uplift people from ignorance and poverty and give them hope for the future.

One of the most articulate writers of that aspiration was Som Nath Zutshi. He began his story writing career under the deep influence of the progressive writers' movement in North India, which was the predominant influence from the 1930s. Urdu writers like Sadat Hasan Manto, Ismat Chughtai and Hindi writers like Premchand and Sudarshan, who were all filled with a social conscience and commitment to bring about a transformation in society. Like them, he too, adopted a simple, naturalistic, totally realistic style of narration. He wrote moving stories about the plight of the down trodden Kashmiris under the feudal, exploitative system; he wrote about their poverty and suffering while holding out hope; these were vividly brought to life in many of his stories.

Later on he, like many talented writers, shook off the influence of the progressive writer. It was no longer possible to believe in the simple idea of human perfectibility. Then other influences from English and European writers began to work and a sophisticated craft of short stories appeared in which Zutshi was one of the pioneers. He acquainted himself with the works of writers like Kafka, Gogol, and others who had moved from realism and introduced the idea of the absurd. Now, his art acquired maturity and a kind of timelessness. So, many of these new stories are a part of this collection and one can see the gradual growth from simplicity to complexity, from emphasis on the externals to a probing of the internal psyche of human beings.

I hope that the true genius of Som Nath Zutshi, one of the foremost Kashmiri writers, will now be recognised by a wider world.

—Neerja Mattoo

Introduction
Innocence to Experience

Som Nath Zutshi is the pioneer of short story writing in Kashmiri language in its modern sense. At the same time, Zutshi's short fiction is the consummation of the development of form during the last seven decades. He has the distinction of having written the first short story in Kashmiri language *Yelyi phol gash* (When the Day Dawned), in 1948 that was published later in *Kong Poash (Saffron Flower)*, the official organ of Kashmir Cultural Front. The story created exciting debate and all agreed that his short story was the most representative form of literature in presenting both individual and collective life determined by economic forces and relations. Many talented Kashmiri writers were already under the influence of Urdu short story writers like Premchand and many others in various languages of the world. Zutshi, the most active among the Progressive writers, continued to write in Kashmiri language. His collection of short stories, titled *Yelyi phol gaash* (When the Day Dawned) was published in 1998, and he got the Sahitya Akademi award for creative writing. The prestigious award was recognition of the development of the genre in Kashmiri language as well as of Zutshi Sahab's contribution to it. Som Nath Zutshi commanded tremendous popularity among the masses for his Radio plays.

Every story contained in the present collection demands a critical approach specific to that story. Nevertheless, all the stories have a common structural approach – to delineate the journey of individual characters from latent innocence to awakened experience. He achieves this excruciating task by representing the character in accordance with his perceptions: No character is known as a particular type or a preordained entity in the immediate reality. The characters are a living force always ready to change and cause changes while residing among others. The individual choices of the characters determine their social demeanor and recognition by others as distinct and tangible reality.

The individuals portrayed in the stories strive to give order and meaning to their lives and of those who concern them. Since strife is the focus of Zutshi, all arbitrary assessments about the characters' ethical and social demeanor are avoided. The writer discovers the individual characters through exploration of the journey, not as ready-made entities already available. Zoon, for instance, in the story *Gith* (The Surge) finds herself completely nonplussed and unable to think of anything other than her condition. Like the inundated banks of the river, she is overwhelmed by the anxiety of having conceived. Her mental state is replicated in the ambient physical reality.

Zoon, who waits painfully for her lover Na'eem, the father of her baby in her womb, discovers herself in a terrifying dilemma when she is encouraged by her friend Noor to get married and experience the ecstasy of married life. She marries a goofy Jamal, but does not feel any joy and faces the horror of social stigma for having pre-marital sex.

Som Nath Zutshi works adroitly through ruminations, sensations, citing common values of moral rectitude and relating mental states with immanent reality to portray the journey from innocence to experience. All his stories are based on ordinary events in the ordinary life of the common people. In each story there is slow but quantitative progression of the making of man; no character is used as a jumble of characteristics, but as a position of unforeseen possibilities in concrete milieu and moment. The characters emerge and grow in particularised geographical, social, and cultural space – called Kashmir, yet they are nevertheless universal in import.

The cultural concerns that shape the behaviour and destiny of common Kashmiri people of various sects, classes and faith, during the last eight decades are seen in continuous change under the changing economic, political, educational and social factors. The stories adequately reflect changes, yet, at the same time, represent various constants in human nature that surface in different kinds of situations. Characters like Fez Dyad and Mohan Lal in *Tears and Food*, Rasul in *When the Day Dawned*, Asha in *Story of a Painting*, Dinanath in the *Vein and the Pain*, Khaliq in *Acquiescence*, and other characters represent various sub-cultures with each sub-culture showing variety under the changes in material aspects of life and the social order.

The characters are shown as being subject to various social and economic factors and have little freedom of choice. At many places there is pathetic surrender to the arbitrary social conformity. For instance, Roopa in *At the Crossroads* surrenders her aspirations and dreams to the prejudice of her mother towards modern education, accepts the fate of a woman who has to live within the four walls of her house in life-long despondence, but wearing the veil of modesty and ruse.

Many stories though replete with vitality, show an inevitable presence of death. Som Nath Zutshi's treatment of death is not elegiac that it terminates life and sends it back to dust, but is different in several contexts. In the story *Guest of One Night*, we find death assuming different roles in the human form. Death appears to frighten human beings who at various stages of their fear try to use it as a stratagem to annihilate others. The young men, metamorphosed into 'Unicorns' as a result of tyranny on them, devise a new way of killing a person who has come to visit the house of his old friend assassinated by them. The victims of one kind of violence accept pain as their destiny, and inflict violence on others while priding themselves in having suffered. 'A nail of steel was driven into his forehead, a wedge like nail. But God's grace, the nail proved to be hollow that blood got congealed within its cavity; not a single drop was spilt'.

Through actions and words the characters engaged in apportioning death to others are shown as miserable and unhappy people in the story. The hidden factors that make the young men agents of spreading death, destruction, and fear actually suffer from unending persecution mania and have an urge for seeking escape from fear. Their morbid propensity for death and decay causes sympathy when the story is read without pre-conceived notions about the type of people. Even the observing protagonist feels the pain of the suffering, but an air of suffocation does not let him scream, and he is advised to remain silent.

In *Acquiescence*, Zutshi uses death as a means of recognition of the forces of circumstances when the protagonist, a Pundit, sitting on the back of a horse, and Khaliq, an elderly person who works as a faithful servant in his family, stop at a spot that reminds them individually of their respective first love and both burst into tears. The story of a day in harsh winter is gradually unfolded through the description of the landscape and the casual conversation between the two characters. The writer adroitly combines the description of landscape, mental states, and conversations about the past and the present of the two characters without any pang of repentance for their remissness in their past. Each of them emerge in his respective social background: The one on the horseback, a well-off person living in the city, and the other holding the bridle of the horse as a poor rustic but contented with his lot. Espying the grave near a spring makes the two characters weep on the sad end of their love. To Khaliq the grave is that of his wife whom he loved passionately, while for the Pundit on the horseback, it is the spot where many years ago he had a romantic escapade with a village girl. Khaliq is not shocked by knowing about the adventure of his boss with the woman buried in the grave; his acquiescence in destiny is un-vacillated.

The beauty of characterisation in Zutshi's stories lies in using sights and scenes of both countryside and urban Kashmir as a background for action. Kashmiri society is depicted without any ideological allegiance, and only through the behaviour of individual characters in unique situations. In all such circumstances men and women tend to protect their momentary as well as permanent individual demands. Unpredictably, they translate their urges into actions against the hostile social order. In *Custody,* the father of a child, namely Ramnath, behaves differently under different impulses without any compunctions; after tantalising his child the whole day by letting him see various items of his desire, he ultimately takes away the money from his hand that he had given him, and hurriedly leaves the house to make his friends happy by buying cinema tickets for them.

Zutshi is known for having introduced social realism in Kashmiri in his maiden story, '*Yelyi phol gash* (When the Day Dawned)'. Later, he continued giving identification to his characters within the changing social order and the associated values and mores of society. However, in some of his stories he skillfully uses surreal incidents and characters to express his experience that deals with the mundane and absurd aspects of reality. Zutshi perceived all characters around him as figments of his own nightmares that moved in consonance with nonsensical and bizarre determining forces, authoritative as well as abhorrently passive.

Those who command authority are shown as nothing but the 'authority – MUST – be obeyed' norm. Stories like *Guest for One Night* and *Chhut chhatak chattak* (Rumbling sound of a train) are and shall remain unparalleled in treating contemporary happenings in the framework of an absurdist approach to life. The powerful men who are leading the life of ennui just like *Poseidon*, busy in causing oceanic upheavals, are shown as inventing trajectories of tyranny. Their dastardly actions, defying explanation, are viewed as stimuli emerging from the deep recesses of the unconscious where they are deeply rooted as dread and a sense of meaninglessness. '…in the posture of praying' at the ridge of the ditch the defenseless captive inwardly feels detached from fears of death, choice, and commitment. The chief of the gang of the Unicorns, momentarily feels elated that his scheme works well and that his cohorts obey him, but, at the same time, he feels wordless sorrow that they might not be able to 'keep the promise'. He is sarcastic about the much repeated statement that 'they are "one"... in the last thousands of years?'

In '*Chhut chhatak chattak*' (Rumblings of the Moving Train), after an eventless wait the passengers in the doomed train have no choice but to accept the fate of the train filled with obnoxious odour that now moves like a huge rugged barge in some rough ocean and then flies like a vulture in the sky. All sorts of people in the ghetto-like train are portrayed to have exercised a wrong choice by undertaking the long journey to escape a precarious situation. The movement of the train is like a ghostly movement as the things surrounding the train show no change; the relativity of motion is felt as vertigo-like inertia. The story could be interpreted differently by various people, but while reading the text, a reader tends to feel like the 'man wearing the white braids' who says, 'All lies! This is the same station where we left from!' Disillusionment with all motivated assurance of freedom and joy is beautifully presented as an allegory of a rumbling train in which the common perdition produces a temporary feeling of fraternity, fellow-being, and a direction towards a common destination.

All eighteen stories in the collection are remarkable for not following any particular style; each has its own technique, language, and approach to understand the idiosyncrasies that are intrinsic to men and women of diverse social backgrounds. Zutshi's language is most natural in the omniscient narrator's speech and also specific to the characters in unique situations. Free from all manner of blithe and unnecessary intellectual impositions, Zutshi's language varies with the aura or mood of the stories and the men and women engaged in them. The description of the atmosphere determines the pervasive feeling aroused by the story. This pliability of fictional language helps the writer to avoid repetition of situations or patterns of character and incidents. Although the eighteen stories in the collection reflect many aspects of contemporary social life of the middle class that emerged after 1947, Zutshi quite deftly manipulates the language in the stories based on fantasy, like *Gung Mahal* (Palace of the Mute).

Nevertheless, the absurdity of the extremes in human nature is depicted within the logic of probability. The king represents the fate of every authoritarian individual who tends to bring all variety and vitality under the frozen and ludicrous designs. Life defies the imposition of arbitrary orders dictated by the phantasmagoria of people who try to shape a variegated social life according to their idiosyncrasies. Deadening silence that aims at quelling every voice to make the sovereign appear as more appalling is ultimately defeated by the myriad voices; heterogeneity of the voices becomes the rule of life: 'The entire city had assembled, but outside the fence of the barbed wire. They all together pulled down the fence and advanced toward the royal palace. Seeing this spectacle, the king swooned and fell down from the window of the highest balcony. The crowd watched him falling and ran toward the carcass of the king. And then there was a cry of victory. The sweet melody of drum and reed-pipes filled the air and the entire city was in rapture' (*Gung Mahal*/Palace of the Mute).

However, in certain situations tumultuous noise is depicted as a social catastrophe that fails all rational thinking; yet it is felt as a contingent happening that affects the social order as well as the individual. In utter helplessness, even uproar is desired as a means of getting salvation. 'If you have courage', one of the characters in *Yim kam Duryodhan* (What Duryodhanas are they?) suggests, 'look toward the sky and raise a unified cry that would smash the dark lid of the sky. Sunlight shall percolate down. If you do not agree, let us keep trudging in the direction of the birds' flight'. In dire and flabbergasting situations one tends to seek help from the unknown.

Employing all the elements of modern fiction – characters, events, conflicts, plot, theme, settings, and points of view - in a harmonious proportion, Zutshi achieves the perfect balance between entertainment and enlightenment. Zutshi needs to be read – re-read – to get the benefit of his life experience, and appreciate his art of powerful expression.

—Shafi Shauq

FEZ, the Grandma

It was my wont to leave office at four in the evening, but today I left rather late. To be exact, it was not quite late, because the order of my promotion was to be handed over to me; wherein they had also increased my salary by Rupees ten. In the meantime, till the order was being signed, I was waiting for my friends and colleagues to come and greet me; it was about five in the evening. Finally, the order was handed over to me with proper signatures, and then I left happily and joyously.

I walked on the road with long steps so I could reach home as early as possible. The times would free us of all our pain and sorrows. After keeping huff, when I show her the order, I would ask her to see it with open eyes and make her realize that she was wrongly proud of her parental kin; Mohammad Ismail too, is no less important, even if she did not acknowledge the same.

I kept thinking about many other things while walking home: 'She might be looking out through the gable to see why her husband was so late. She might be watching, and as soon as I reached the entrance of the alley, I would look at her with a smile. The moment I enter the house, I would go up running and stop in the gables. All my kith and kin shall throng around me.'

While my mind was busy with such thoughts, I hardly knew when I crossed the bridge and reached near my house. I stopped at the entry of the alley, raised my eyes up towards the gable and found the window was shut. I walked a couple of steps further and heard loud shrieks coming from the house on our right. All my verve petered out, my legs slowed as if they were out of joints and, with slow steps, I entered my house.

'I wish your limbs get hamstrung! You dare to slap me?' I heard Fez cursing the son of her daughter. She had raised a lot of din. 'I wish you get blind! You make me suffer. Oh my God!'

I understood there was a new kind of broil; the shut window of the gable made my guess stronger. I was finally convinced that Fez was a vampire who would devour all her kindred one by one and yet remain hungry. How cruelly she treats that little five year old child - inflicting all manner of pain on him! Doing so, she deprives all in the neighbourhood of their peace and pleasure. With white hair, a long nose on her elongated face, a maze of furrows on her forehead she is senseless like a wall. She possesses a tongue that pulverizes even iron, not to speak of humans - whosoever she meets. A dirty wretch!

I calmly entered my house and felt all my senses were out of gear. Holding my knees with my hands, I somehow climbed up the stairs and reached the gable room. I opened the door of my room and stepped in. Not even a dog met me. And how could anyone? They had hid themselves in holes from the fright of the roaring monster.

'Do you think that you or your father are the only ones who hate me? All others in the world hate me. Even the neighbours detest me...'

On hearing this, I shuddered. I felt there was a fire in the vicinity that was spreading towards our house, ready to engulf it. Thus, I called in a rather low voice,

'Haleema!'

Haleema appeared before me like a frightened cat. Her face evinced me, 'Do you hear what rubbish she utters?'

'What is the issue, my daughter?'

'We did not say anything to provoke her. Boba says that we have kept the windows shut. Subhana made her bleed through the nose. Then she started pulling her own hair. He was insisting for something from her.'

And soon my wife also appeared there. While quivering she heaved a deep sigh. 'Thank God she forgave us and now she has calmed down. Haleema, will you please keep water for boiling to make tea? The Earthen oven has already some wood splinters in it. But take care that you do not open the window for now.' Holding her face in her hands she sat grouchily in a corner. I thought of breaking the good news to her so she felt cheerful, but Fez was struck almost deaf. In the meantime, my eagerness to tell her the good word had somewhat faded and thus I asked her,

'Did you open that window? She was frenzied against us only.'

She moved her head to show 'no'.

'Do you remember how vengeful she was against us when she held her son Subhana by his ears and pushed him to tumble down the stairs and I watched it and gave a shriek? I had dared to say to her, "Fez, do not be so cruel to him. Don't you feel any pity for him?" Hearing my words she was angered and pounced on me like an angry she-monkey. Since that day whenever she thrashes him, we shut our window.'

And it was true. Not only we, but all the folks in our neighbourhood shut their windows. 'Has her son-in-law not returned from his work-place?' I asked my wife.

'Not yet. But I am sure, she will wear an altogether different mood until he returns.' My wife said to me.

Kareem Khan, a simple and naive guy, was Fez's son-in-law. He was a mason and left his house early in the morning and returned late in the evening with his emptied tiffin box. When Kareem Khan's wife died, Subhana was just a breastfed child. She was the only daughter of Fez who Kareem Khan got to his own home after her death; he hoped that she would at least take care of the toddler. But since the day we shifted to this house we observed her inflicting all kinds of physical torture on him. From dawn to dusk, she was stubborn and would beat the boy.

My wife stood up and said, 'Now she has calmed down.'

In the meantime, Fez was heard saying, 'Subhana! Subhana! Where are you?'

I said to my wife in a low voice, 'You know her temperament thoroughly, isn't it?'

She smiled and went to the cooking area. I thought the condition was favourable to break the good news to her.

'Listen!' I said to her.

'Wait a while.' She replied. 'Let me place the rice pot on the oven.'

It was almost evening. I heard the sound of the opening window and peeped through a vent. It was Fez looking at the window of our cooking area. After a while, she called,

'Zeba! Zeba!'

'Yes. What?' My wife asked her without opening the window. She looked at me and hinted with the motion of her head and feigned to be busy by striking the grinding pot as if she was pounding spices.

'Did Subhana come to your house?' Fez asked my wife.

'No sister, he did not.' My wife replied.

'Who knows where he has gone?' Fez muttered to herself. Then there was silence for some moments.

'Zeba!...Zeba!' Fez called again.

'What is it now, sister?'

'Why are you hiding behind your closed windows? It appears you are hiding your chastity. Or is it that my foes have talked bad about me to you?'

My wife implied that Fez tried to instigate her. If she opened the window, it was difficult for them to look at each other. And if she did not do so, her snake-like words might keep her biting. She anon opened the door, pasted a false smile on her face and said to her, 'Sister, I was busy with crushing a few red chillies.'

'What are you cooking for today's meals?'

She was yet to receive a reply when some noise was heard in the street.

'What is that bevy about near the lamp-post?' She craned half her body out to see. My wife too glimpsed something at the entrance of the street. I, too, heard some noise and opened my window to look out. Fez again espied me and withdrew from her sill.

She tidied her head-cover as she always behaved like that, and I always thought it was weird. I looked at the entrance of the street, and saw a veiled woman sitting near the lamp-post, and people standing around her. I ran down the stairs and wriggled through the crowd. I saw the veiled woman crying and shedding tears.

'What is the matter, dear?' I asked a spectator.

'She has lost her son.' He said to me. 'She has not been able to find him since 2.00 pm. See, her eyes have turned red by shedding tears.'

'Yes. Why not? There can be nothing more painful

than losing a child.' Another person standing there commented. The third bystander said to me, 'Isn't it true, Sir?' I was at a loss of words. The onlookers were neighbours to one another and left the site by holding each other's shoulders. They twitched one another and laughed secretly. I looked back and found Fez was worming her way through the crowd.

'What is the issue, sister?' She asked the veiled woman who was lachrymose. 'Is anything wrong with you?'

'Her son is missing since afternoon.' A guy reported to her.

'What is there to worry about? He will be home on his own. Do not grieve like that.' She consoled the veiled woman.

On reaching the roadside, she called out, 'Subhana! Subhana! Come here. Let my life be sacrificed for you! Come, come back.'

When she returned, she again said to the tearful veiled woman. 'You need not worry. He will return on his own. If you have cattle - forget cattle, if you have... or a cockerel that too is home in the evening.'

A woman of the neighbourhood felt agitated and said indirectly to Fez, 'Do not torment the poor woman for she alone knows what irks her. You just keep talking. Get up now, my sister, let's report the matter to the police. You make vague suggestions! Her son is just a five-year old. My God!'

And then darkness set in. It could be that, 'God save him, somebody has stifled him'.

Initially Fez was about to quarrel for anger was visible in her eyes, but then she quivered. She felt her kin was chilled. She came out from the bevy and walked to the roadside. She called in her highest pitch,

'Subhana! Subhana!!'

Subhana looked at her secretly from the entry of another alley.

'Come Subhana! Let me sacrifice myself for you! Come, I might give my life for your well-being! I have no energy left in my body.'

Then Fez walked towards that spot, and seeing this, he started fleeing.

'Come dear, come now.'

As soon as he ran, she ran after him like a mad woman.

'Come, I wish death seized you! Let you be trampled under the wheels of some *tonga!* What has possessed you? Some rogue might strangle you there!'

Hearing these cries from Fez, all gazed at her.

Tears and Food

'A bottle of medicine and wool for Prabha, an embroidered shirt and footwear for Nana, a coat for myself .... No, it is too much. I do not have so much money.'

'A bottle of medicine for Prabha, an embroidered shirt and footwear for Nana, a coat for myself... No, that hardly makes any difference.'

'An embroidered shirt and footwear for Nana, a bottle of medicine for Prabha... Yes, that makes some difference.'

It was payday, and Mohan Lal was busy making estimates of the expenses. He had moved the typewriter to the corner of his table, and was making a list of all the expenses for the month on a scroll of paper. Now he was deciding what all could be purchased after clearing the debts of the month. He finally decided not to go in for a coat for himself. 'My little daughter should get covered first, and then my ailing wife, she has to recover; I am not the issue.'

As soon as he finished the calculations, he heard some kind of hubbub in the big room off the office. He got up, looked through the door, and saw the cashier carrying a bagful of money; all the employees were waiting for him. It was past 4 pm and all were waiting for him to come. As soon as they saw him, they started jostling to grab the first turn to receive the pay. There were a few who laughed and sniggered at one another.

Mohan Lal too, joyously came out of his room and joined the other employees. He wriggled through the bevy to be the first to receive his salary, and then left the office. But the joy he felt before receiving his salary was lost. In the meantime, he had remembered another lender who he had not included in his estimate. He felt huffed and his face blushed; he started making a new estimate:

A bottle of medicine for Prabha, an embroidered footwear for Nana ....that is all for this time; let other things be postponed to next month. However, he felt that the coming month was much longer – not less than 31 days. Waiting for 31 days was a big torment.

He was lost in rumination when he looked at the door. He saw Sarwanand, keeping one foot inside the room, and the other outside, busy in counting the notes, for he did not need money for anything; he had already amassed much by doing sycophancy of the officer and swindling. 'And then he hardly had any expenses to bear, he neither needs clothes nor food items. I wish he would give all that money to me so I could fulfil some needs. He would be having a lot of money!' The thin cotton parrot-coloured turban that he wore on his head had many streaks of dirt, and each streak evinced that he possessed no less than Rupees One thousand.

In the room amidst the din, somebody's distinct guffaw could be heard. This incensed Sarwananad, 'God forgive them! They are not even letting me count properly. They are worse than the penurious labourers. How loud are their voices! If boss happens to come here without notice, he will transfer them to remote areas.' He counted his money again, and then put it in the concealed pocket of his garment. He looked around to see if he had dropped anything, and then left.

Mohan Lal smiled again when he remembered Sarwanand's words; a while ago he had made fun of Sarwanand which had upset him and he had said, 'You a new recruit! Do you scoff me? Let the bad times be damned that these lads with perfumed oil in their hair are usurping all. You are still a novice, but you get double my salary, so you think you have the right to laugh at others. You would know the value of money if you spent your whole life in serving.'

Sarwanand's words had hurt Mohan Lal's heart. He apprehended that he too might have to face what Sarwanand was facing. I wish I was not forced to do what Sarwanand did. 'But why? I am not inefficient like him.' He prided in being a B.A. of his time. He was also proud of being able to write good drafts that had to some extent endeared him to his boss.

After having discussed all this with himself, he returned to his list of expenditure: 'An embroidered shirt for Nana, a bottle of medicine for Prabha...' While repeating this mantra he left the office as he decided to go home after purchasing the items.

When he entered his house in the evening, he carried the packages under both his armpits: a bottle of medicine for Prabha, embroidered shirt for Nana, wool, foot-cover, and cloth for his coat.

'Nana! Dear daughter Nana, come, see what pretty shoes I have for you!' Mohan Lal wasted no time to say this as he was home.

Mohan Lal's wife Prabhaji was busy in stitching a shirt. Seeing her husband in a happy mood, she too felt happy. With a smile on her lips, she said to him, 'She is sleeping. Let her sleep not be disturbed.'

Mohan Lal dropped the packets in front of Prabha.

She felt happy to see the items, but soon gave a deep sigh. Her face showed sudden withering as Mohan Lal's face had withered soon after receiving his salary. Her husband expected her to be happy after receiving the money and then assess each item that he had got home, but Prabhaji sensed the serpents and vipers in them; she was scared to touch them.

'Please check each item one by one to see if it is good,' Mohan Lal said with a smiling visage. 'Why are you struck dumb?'

Parabhaji still maintained her silence. However, to please her husband she pulled the goods closer to her.

'Now take the things; you should be happy, I beseech you.' He said to her with a piteous look.

'We too have our god! Let's wait and see what he decides in our favour. I can see that you are happy, though inwardly.'

Heaving a sigh, Prabhaji said to him, 'Yes, Why not? After all whatever you decide is fine. Yet, I had asked you to get some knitting wool as well. After all, Nana was not in need of any shoes. And then who are my well-wishers that I would go to them for any feasts? But, how can I go anywhere without a sweater? What did I do without a sweater till date?'

Her mention of "well-wishers" convinced Mohan Lal that this might lead to some new nagging. But she changed her mood instantly and said smilingly, 'Go on doing your cons. I know how clever you are. We will get enough money within a day or two, if Bhagwan wishes so.' Feeling a little happy, Prabhaji said further, 'Did anything come about of that award?'

'That is what I meant to tell you. I shall certainly get the award. You may blame me if I do not get it. I filled the form for Tiku on that day. Didn't he get it?'

Feeling better, Prabhaji assessed the items one by one.

'This cloth must have been very costly? Isn't it?' She asked him.

Mohan Lal feared that she might get grievous again, so he hastened to say, 'No, not quite costly; it costs just Rupees Three a yard.'

Prabhaji was lugubrious again. She wanted him to get rid of his old coat which was threadbare from the elbows, and buy a new coat for himself, but she also thought of all the lenders.

Prabhaji said to him, 'I want you to return all these things and keep just the cloth for the coat. You are after all an office going person, you must buy a new coat for yourself.'

She then thrust her hand into the pocket of her blouse, and got a couple of scraps which she handed over to Mohan Lal.

'Here are the bills of the provision stores. You have to pay money to them. And the wood seller has come four times since morning. Oh yes, Sarwanand also came here, I don't know why.'

The mention of the bills did not affect Mohan Lal, but being reminded of the wood vendor made him anxious as he had had an abusive altercation with him last month. Thus, Mohan Lal moaned when he recollected: payday and abuses, the bag and the bullet, rejoicing and grieving. He felt very angry and frustrated. He had counted each day to get his pay. He stared silently at all the items he had fetched. His eyes twitched, but he assumed it was the flickering of the electric lamp.

Prabhaji observed that he became grieved by the mention of the bills. In order to console him, she said, 'I swear by Nana, please get all these items only when you get the prize. And then you can get me a Bangaloru *Dhoti* as well.'

On hearing her swearing by Nana, and mentioning the prize, he really felt sanguine. He said to her, 'I will not have any trouble then. Not only a Bangaloru dhoti, but I will also get you ear-pendants. Then I will be able to clear all the debts. Today, I will make a new resolution and then think of tomorrow.'

'Let me see what you gained from the previous one.' Prabhaji was not taken in by his words – The prize and then her husband!

Mohan Lal felt hurt by his wife's words. He felt all alone, seeking sympathy from his wife; he had surrendered his arsenal. He tried to get approval for whatever he said and with this hope he looked at his wife. He found her looking askance at him. He said to her, 'You see this time, I swear by Nana, I expect to get it in a couple of days.' Thus Mohan Lal consoled himself, more than that he consoled his wife. She felt a little happy, and seeing her happy, Mohan Lal also felt happy. Seeing the smiling lips of Prabhaji, Mohan Lal was out of bounds with joy.

He sat propped up against the wall. He ruminated again and made details of the money he expected to get as a prize; he felt the bliss of paradise. He felt himself climbing up the steps of colourful mansions, and while he pondered, his eyes glistened with pleasure and his face shone anew with hopes.

Prabhaji sat aside and busied herself in stitching a worn out shirt. Now and then she shifted her eyes from her stitching needle to her husband.

Just then the door of the house creaked open. Prabhaji

hurried to look through the window, and then retired to her private closet. Mohan Lal was taken aback when he found Sarwanand standing before him.

'Mohanji, what are you pondering about?' While sitting down, Sarwanand asked him. 'What a torture! This is my second turn.'

Thus, he got Mohanji back from his fantasy.

'What made you come to see me, Sarwa Kak?' Mohan Lal asked him smilingly.

'Me? Why did I come? Take this and keep it safely.' Saying this, he took out a bundle of notes from his interior pocket and placed it in front of Mohan Lal.

Mohan Lal did not waste any time in catching hold of the bundle of notes. He uttered abruptly,

'Prabha! Prabha! Come fast. Didn't I tell you a little while ago that we shall receive it in a day or so? Come, and see, the prize money is here.' He was about to shout, and laugh to himself. He tried to make Sarwanand understand: 'This is what they say: "ask for something and get it anon!"'

Sarwanand was befuddled and said to him, 'First you count it, and then shout.'

But Mohan Lal did not want to count the money at that moment, for it could take some time. He kept the bundle of notes firmly clasped in his two hands, and was about to run to the inner closet to show it to his wife, but Sarwanand took hold of his arm, and made him sit down. Mohan Lal was about to climb up the mansion of his dreams, but Sarwanand pulled his leg from behind and made him step down.

"Mohan Lal, it is a sum of Rupees Five hundred. The boss wants you to deposit the money in Lloyd's Bank. Here is the slip.'

The bundle of notes slipped from his hands and he stood flabbergasted. Prabhaji came out of her private closet.

Seeing drops of tears in her husband's eyes, she hung her head gloomily.

What Duryodhanas are they?

A huge hullabaloo was heard. And wouldn't it be? It was almost the doomsday, the Day of Judgement. In broad daylight the sky was overcast with darkness as if with a black sheet of polythene. Nothing but two hirsute hands were visible that were busy in spreading the black polythene. Initially, the Sun was eclipsed, its volume dwindled, and finally it started vanishing. It left a black dot behind, then that too disappeared. It appeared like a starless night.

A huge hullabaloo was heard.

People shut their doors and windows. 'Is this what they call the Doomsday?'

Darkness flowed in to fill the rooms, they switched the electric lamps, but there was no light. Then they took out their old lamps, but they could not be lit. Besides, it was very chilly. Mothers kept their little ones in tight embraces. They gave out loud shrieks, not exactly weeping cries, as there was hardly any strength in the cries.

The crows flocking southwards on the uplands, searching for grains and leftover spikes in fields and on ridges, were astounded. They too crowed loudly, but soon some mysterious intuition made them unable to sense the smell of the night. They thronged at one place and raised a din. 'This is not any real night.' The crows flew in multitudes and took on wings. They could not be seen, only the hissing flapping of their wings evinced they turned towards the North to take refuge in their nests and hiding places. Nobody knew where they flew to, and many of them fell to the ground.

In the meantime, a loud call was heard, 'Take care, be awake!' The doors were banged with sticks. Some people called out, but those who were stricken with fear showed a little life again to understand that men are still alive.

And then there was again a large hullabaloo.

People in bevy in the open fields showed their faces smashed, and many more were seen without life. One among the crowd said aloud, 'Guys, please do not get frightened for it is not a real night. The dark blanket spread all over shall be removed and there shall be light again!'

Some other person said, 'False! The Sun has finally fled away. How long could life forms live?'

The first one said in reply, 'Remember, how in the *Mahabharata* nightfall happened in the afternoon. Do not get frightened.'

The second one replied, 'That night, for an hour or

so, was the result of Lord Krishna's stratagem to perish falsehood. This night of today is lengthened for so many hours. Where shall we see Krishna who could wrap all this night into a skein? The present night is more formidable than the one in the *Mahabharata*.'

Some third person said, 'It is true that Lord Krishna cannot have reincarnated. And how can he come to remove the wrapping of darkness when it is already the *Kalyuga*?'

Then some fourth voice was heard saying, 'Listen, Oh my brothers! Do not waste any more time. All the souls shall peter out very soon. Let's run fast towards the direction that all the flying birds fled to. Hear the hissing sound of their flapping wings *sa-sa-sa*... Millions of them have fled'.

Thus, they all agreed and left.

Again a new hullabaloo was raised.

The mothers, with their babies clung to their breasts, also fled along with thousands of people. Their cries were hardly audible over the breathing sounds. The harshness of the chill hardly let them have an inkling of what condition their children were in. They in fact, did not think whether their children still breathed.

All the fleeing people kept crooning while they moved like a wave. 'If any one falls during the journey, do not mind, keep moving ahead!'

'How many of us will reach there?'

This question was hardly answered when a calm sound of *Keertana* (Religious hymn) was heard and it felt that they were in the middle of a jungle; a sage might be residing there, they thought.

'Who is there?'

'*SHSHSH...* be quiet! A sage is wrapped in Yoga there.' The question got a reply.

'Will he keep performing Yoga till the whole world perishes? Convey to him that life on the Earth is ending. Exhibit the power of your *Shakti*, but do it now!'

The sage heard these words, and evinced a smile on his lips. He then said from a distance, 'This is the result of our sins and nothing more than that. It is the fruit of your bad deeds that you endure. Now enter this endlessly long grotto, pray for you absolution, and achieve freedom!'

The second voice in the bevy said, 'O blessed sage! We have hardly had any time to live this worldly existence. You say that all humans in the world are sinners and that they could attain salvation only through sacrificing their lives!'

The third voice said, 'O blessed Saint, tell us why did Brahma create the creations? He never intended to finish the world before its natural end. No icon-maker makes his icons only to break them. He created the Sun, the Moon, the stars, and the Earth not with the intention of destroying it all. Why should He disturb the balance of the cosmos? Impossible.'

The first voice said rather aloud, 'O blessed Seer! You say that gloom shall overwhelm light? The war of Mahabharata shall be repeated and Duryodhana will win? Falsehood shall make Truth famished for a drop of water? O Maharaja, the sinners are very few like unhusked grains in husked rice; a fly in a cauldron of milk. Why don't you punish only such sinners? We wish we could attain freedom in this birth only.'

Hearing this, the sage gave out a big guffaw in self-mortification; he was in ire. He started panting in rage and said, 'This is the delusion of Maya! Only the name of God shall abide.'

One among the people replied, 'But there shall be no one left to say His name! The manifest implies impossible.'

The people again raised their voices. One said, 'Was not Duryodhana succoured by the saints?'

The second voice said, 'He, himself, is seeking liberation from life! How could he help others?'

'If you have courage, look towards the sky and raise a unified cry that will smash the dark lid of the sky. Sunlight shall percolate down. If you do not agree, let us keep trudging in the direction of the birds' flight.'

Again a cacophony of sound was heard.

A loud shriek was heard coming out of the house near the field from where they had started their journey; it was a male's shriek. All of a sudden, he sprang up from his cot and quivered. His eyes were dazed by a bright light that made him rub his eyes. His mother came running from the adjacent room, saying, 'Why did you scream? I was frightened.'

'Did my scream sound like a courageous scream, or...?'

His mother could not make anything of what he said.

He got up abruptly, opened the glass panes of the window. The heaps of withered leaves in the kitchen garden appeared like small scraps of black polythene; but the lonely rose bush was intact. He recovered the hue of his face. Morning was in the offing, yet he bore a longing in his mind, 'I wish I could see all the crows returning to their nests in the evening with loud flaps.'

He then returned to his cot. 'How many more Duryodhans will take rebirth in the coming days?' He pondered.

When the Day Dawned

It was snowing in plenty for the last two days; no end to it could be envisaged. When one looked upward into the sky, it appeared as if minute swarthy insects were descending down in swarms. Looking towards the nearby houses, the flakes looked like big skeins of cotton. Fancy suggested that a carder was there in the sky endlessly carding fluffy cotton and sending it down to the Earth. Or, it could be as if in spring the petals of pear blossoms were shaken from the trees of Kashmir and put together in a dense copse. Yester evening the layer of snow was sparse and patchy, but in the morning it had become dense and smooth. It was snowing so densely that visibility was just ten to twenty yards. Beyond that was thick fog and smoke; the Sun was about to set.

Having worked for the whole day, Rasool was walking towards his home. A tattered blanket, thoroughly drenched, covered him like a cap-a-pie. Taking long strides he trudged through the snow. He was free from work a little earlier for it was snowing continuously. And then there was not much to do at Lalaji's shop; the huge bundles were to be moved and kept in order, as all would get ruined by snow. Secondly, Lalaji was making preparations to celebrate the Republic Day, and had sent Rasool to the potter's colony to fetch earthen lamps. Besides, he had also been asked to buy cotton wicks for the carder, oil and sweets from the confectionary. He had also ordered some necessary things from the milkman. When Rasool accomplished all these chores nicely, Lalaji looked at him and said in appreciation:

'So you have finished all the tasks as directed?'

Lalaji had been doing his business in Kashmir for years; though he hailed from Amritsar. While interacting with the locals, he had acquired conversational skills in the vernacular.

'Have you got all the essential goods?'

'Yes, my master, I got you all the things you asked.' Coming closer to Lalaji, he said 'Will you please get that *chilim* (tobacco-pot) of the hookah nearer?' But Lalaji was again engrossed in his accounts. Therefore, Rasool stretched his arm, got the *chilim*, took a few long puffs of smoke, and placed the pot again on the hookah with a long serpent-like pipe.

'Master, all my fingertips are numb with cold.' He said to Lalaji. 'And my son is sick at home. Can you let me leave a little early, please?' But Lalaji was still busy, not evincing even a little movement of his lips. It appeared he was imprecating cockerel-thieves.

Rasool got no reply to his entreaty from his master. Yet he kept staring at him. But Rasool did not have that intense eyesight as he used to have in the past. Of late, his eyes had developed some kind of intensity and hate. In the past, he could hardly dare to look at his master's face. At the most, he could get fascinated by looking at his master's dress, the drooping shawl on his shoulders, his serpent like smoking pipe, his round pillow, the bed-cover..., but now he could discern all: sewing and wearing, black and white, ... And Lalaji, too, could grasp that someone has instigated his loyal servant.

It was snowing, and Lalaji was engaged in his calculations. Rasool looked at his feet in the very cheap grass-shoes (*Pulhore*) and as such got red due to the chill and caused vapour, and then cast a look at Lalaji's face.

'Do you hear me, Sir? May I leave a little earlier today?' Rasool asked him again.

Lalaji turned his neck and said, 'Yes, what did you say? Leave? ... Okay, you may leave now, but remember, be on duty earlier than usual tomorrow.'

'Sure Sir. I'll, provided my son is well.'

'How is he feeling now? You should make him drink hot water so that his fever comes down. I wish God cures him soon.'

After saying salaam and good wishes, Rasool walked towards his home. Wearing a soggy blanket from head to feet, he strode homewards. 'Yesterday, Lalaji knew it well what an auspicious day it was tomorrow,' he kept thinking. 'India was to achieve her freedom, and would be truly free to become a republic.' But he also thought that if it was really true that tomorrow is such an important day, then why didn't Samad Kak, Jamal Dar and Qadir Sheikh tell him so yesterday. Every evening, they would all meet and talk about problems at the factory, difficulties of the artisans and labourers' conditions. Why did they keep it secret from him?'

Rapt in such musings, he reached Amira Kadal. He saw many military vehicles passing over the bridge. The *Tonga* drivers kept their horses bridled to make them pace slowly. The road labourers had cut both sides of the mass of snow so that the horses would not skid. It was the day of parade for the army the next day. There were no beggars on the footpaths, all had left their places. Most of these beggars came from Gurez and Tilel, who had fled their homes during the raids of the tribal fighters; all others had dwindled in numbers. Only a little cute girl was left behind.

Rasool crossed the bridge and saw the girl sitting on snow under the roof extension of a shop. She kept the skirt of her garment spread. A street-vender was also there near her. While talking to each other, the girl knew that a military parade was scheduled for the next day. She also knew that all the people were going to be free, completely free. Rasool stopped for a while near the street vendor, conversing about his well-being. The girl took a chance and said to Rasool, 'May my Prophet set you and your kindred free! Give me a paisa, please!'

While Rasool looked at her, an army truck wriggled through the snow and filled the skirt of the girl with snow. Rasool felt bad to see it; something came to his mind and speeded up his pace. He wore his wet blanket tighter to his body and didn't look behind. He knew it was very late although he had left the shop earlier. He remembered that his son was ill, and that he was expected to be home as early as possible. He again thought about the condition of his ailing son. Thoughts about being a servant to a businessman, and the daily hard labour filled his mind. It was really hard to eke out.

However, the snowfall allowed him a little free time. 'How could I arrange for his evening meals? How could I fetch liquorices and other herbal medicines for him that the aged neighbour Wahab Sahab had suggested for his relief from cold? And there was also no medicine seller nearby. How could I carry my son in high fever? ... I consulted the doctor, but he asked me to get my son there. Let me take him to the doctor the day after tomorrow... Tomorrow is our Republic Day. I entreated the doctor to examine him, but he told me that he could not see any patient as all were going to celebrate the Republic Day...'

On nearing his house, his anxieties increased, for he was the unlucky fellow who was nearly a pauper, and faced many misfortunes; he did not even want to enter his house. He didn't want to go in as he would be asked if he had got anything for the family. Kids would come weeping to him, all shivering with cold and hunger, and others were sick. However, Rasool was quite caring and despite the many hardships, never gave in. On entering the threshold he remembered all. It was already dusk, and the sparrows and mynas had already gone into their warm nests because the heavy snowfall hardly gave them time to venture out; they too were dumbstruck.

On entering the door, he shook off the snow from his snow-covered blanket; it was so drenched that it could be squeezed. It had stopped snowing, but when he walked up the stairs of his two-storey shanty, he saw water trickling down from the roof which had many holes. The snow was melting and water was pouring through the many vents.

There in a dark corner of the room lay his sick son under a sparse cover. Bieb, too, was sitting mute and weary beside him; she looked like the flame of a dry oil lamp about to extinguish. When Bieb saw that her husband was home, she felt a little energised. With a glimmer of hope on her face she felt spirited. Rasool raised his eyes to yet another corner and saw his other son and a little daughter lying dumbly there.

'What was his condition during the day?' Rasool asked his wife. 'Did he take the syrup?'

'Only a few sips, that too on insisting.' She replied.

They were barely talking about the ailing boy when he coughed violently. The phlegm in his chest produced wheezing. 'Oh father!' He whined.

'Yes, my dear son? How do you feel now?' Saying this Rasool placed his hand on his chest. He felt his heart beating fast like a dying person in his throes. His fever was high and he gasped for breath.

Bieb looked at her husband and then at him.

'It is quite normal with children to fall sick and suffer from cold. There is nothing to worry about.' Rasool tried to calm his wife.

'But he has been like this for so many days! I hope nothing strikes me!' She sighed.

Drops of water trickled down in the third corner of the room. The wick of the earthen oil-lamp needed trimming. Rasool calmly went near the lamp and removed the ashes from the tip. Then he asked Bieb, 'Did Samad Kak come here?'

'Yes, and Jamal Kaka and Qadir Sheikh were also with him.'

'What did they say?'

'They said that Rasool did not mention Sula's sickness. And then they gossiped with each other. They assured me that they would come again in the morning along with the doctor. They tried to get him today, but he did not agree to come. Obviously, it was already nine o'clock and then it was snowing.'

'Hahahaha… Now please get up and make him sip a little syrup.'

Bieb sighed again, and said, 'Yes, let me get up. Oh my God! Our country and the world have got freedom, but we alone have not come out of this misery!'

'Hahahah… What could God do?' said Rasool.

Bieb somehow or the other made Sula take half a cup of syrup. Then each of them ate a couple of morsels of rice.

Bieb handed over a smeared quilt to Rasool, and nestled close to her ailing son Sula. Rasool stretched out holding an old *kaangri* beside him. Feeling very cold, he could not sleep easily. He turned, and espied the lamp that made him shudder. His anxiety increased and he recollected many forgotten things. On one hand, tomorrow was the Republic Day, and on the other hand, he remembered the day when his son fell ill. He had a harsh bickering with Bieb. Remembering that day, he grew penitent for she had to face his wrath for no fault of hers. She did not make him fall ill, he thought.

The innocent child had slipped in the compound which drenched all his rags in mire. She removed his clothes, but there was no alternative clothing to cover his body and thus he had to remain naked for over an hour which made him ill. … Recollecting all these events, Rasool heaved a long sigh. Then he also had a bout of ire by recollecting what Lalaji had told him about freedom. 'Do his kids, too, get ill like that? Does he too face imprecations at his home? Do they too slip in the mud? Had they no car of their own, then they too would undoubtedly slip in the mud. ... When there is a fall, one is sure to get injured. … But we forbear and then stand up again. … If they have a fall, they might never be able to stand again. …

'If he was angered a few days ago, then why did he talk calmly later? …How long can he succeed in his clever ways? I asked him for Rupees Five as advance, with the entreaty that my son is not well, and he flatly refused…

as if my entreaty would take his life. ... It is really not a big deal to take their life....If they sense the loss of even half a paisa, their faces get insipid. ... They have no want in any manner. He owns a couple of factories, although in partnership with Khwaja Sultan. And then he gets commission for running his agency. He has five vehicles of his own that transport material from Amritsar which his brother sends ...' He continued ruminating.

The lamp dimmed. The room was filled with silence. Only the barking of dogs outside made the silence quiver. All of a sudden Bieb awoke. 'Rasool! Are you awake?' She called him rather calmly.

'Yes. Are you well?' Rasool asked her.

'I feel frightened... I had a dream...'

'Hahahaha... Sleep and take rest... Please see if Sula's fever has come down.'

Bieb stretched her arm to feel Sula's fever. The two glass bangles made a slight tinkle.

'He still has fever, but it seems a little less. I had a horrid dream.'

Rasool made a slight laugh, but Bieb quickly swore: 'I swear by God, I had a frightening dream. Did they not say that there would be a procession in Delhi tomorrow? That is what I dreamed. A huge crowd was there in the procession. Many women were beating their chests. I asked them, 'Sisters, why do you wail?' 'We can't find our children here; we fear they might get trammelled in the crowd. See even the grown-ups get mashed under the feet'. I said in reply, 'Sister, my son is not well. When we celebrated the victory of the Maharaja in our Kashmir, we watched the courtly procession. Our son went in a little canoe to join a bevy of kids of the boatmen to see the spectacle. The waves caused by the powerboats pushed their canoes behind. Many *shikaras* were even sunk. Sister, I too used to lament like you.'

When Bieb finished narrating her dream, Rasool reflected, 'How could you know? You dreamed of a freedom procession and people getting crushed under feet, but that moment has not ended here yet; I still bear the after-shock of that stampede in my mind. The only difference is that nowadays that wave takes all in its sway while the same spate proves a spate of money for Lalaji and people like him.'

Rasool was again agitated when he recollected what Lalaji had said to him about freedom. He could find no way to sleep. He kept tossing and turning and had disturbing thoughts. Then he thought of an important thing: 'If Lalaji's words are true, then my prediction too must prove true', he thought.

While he was still tossing and turning, the day dawned. Bieb too woke up. She felt Sula's chest and was relieved to find his heart beating slower than yester night, and his wheezing too had subsided a little. His fever had come down.

'Is he feeling better than yesterday?' Rasool asked her in his perplexity.

'Yes, by God's kindness, he is feeling better than yesterday. I hope he shall be soon free from his pain.'

Bieb told him. Saying this she rose and spread the quilt over her two kids. Then she went to the cooking place to brew a hot cup of tea for her husband.

Rasool opened the window and saw it was still snowing, even heavier than yesterday. Over six inches thick layer of snow had covered everything. It appeared dark even after the dawn of the day. Snowflakes did not appear like swarms of minute insects, but like locusts to devour all. The flakes might be getting amassed on Lalaji's bungalow like petals of pear blossoms.

It was smoggy just as it was yesterday; the eyes could not see distant things, neither to the right nor to the left, neither forward nor backward. He felt the whole humanity was in shackles; the broad roads and the electric cables appeared like white tethers, or iron chains that kept all his family and kith and kin tied. Life appeared to have frozen. Rasool grew restless and got up.

'Bieb!' He called his wife.

'Yes!' Bieb came almost running. 'What happened? Where are you going?'

'I am going to Amira Kadal. We will have *Qahva* (*green tea)* when I am back.'

'But Samad Kak and Qadir Sheikh too are about to join you. The doctor cannot keep waiting for you.' Bieb said to him.

'I shall take them along. I cannot do without them. We may think of the doctor later.' Rasool replied.

'What errand is so important and urgent?' Bieb asked in surprise.

Rasool stared at her as if he was gathering his own dispersed ideas from her face; weird ideas, weird desires and yearnings, all put together strengthened his resolution. One resolution…

While looking at Bieb's face, he said ruminating, 'It is really a contingency. It needs getting accomplished …I shall be set free… The lamp will not die for want of oil… The English fled, but the snow is not yet melting… If Lalaji is big, what makes us less? The little ones too must grow. The one in a cradle cannot always remain there. Sula too, shall grow one day… if he lives. HAHAHA! He has the right to live. Independent people do not die so easily. Why do the young ones of the West not die? The English! Fraudulent people! Why don't you know? Innumerable swindlers! They play tricks to suck out our lives. They loot and slay us; the labour is ours, the courage is ours, the determination is ours! They cannot divest us of our courage, no, they cannot.'

Rasool was in fury and started roaring. His lips and ears quivered. 'The swindlers cannot remain here anymore. Sula shall surely live! Samad Kak's Amma shall live! Qadir Sheikh's Jaan will live!' Uttering such words, Rasool was leaving, while Bieb stared at him with amazement.

People had already made paths through the snow by trampling over it to reach the bigger roads and alleys. However, they were still covered with plain snow as nobody had come outdoors. Rasool was the first human being who made a bridle path in his lane that joined the bigger road. He thought of all the small paths; the paths of independent people who had liberated humanity from getting confined by fetters, who had saved life from getting frozen.

Rasool looked upwards to see snow mounds dropping from the hanging electric wires. He envisioned that all the white tethers were broken. He was sure in his fancy that this, this alone was the path to freedom. He plodded at a faster pace through the snow.

Chhut Chhatak Chhatak
The Chugging of a Train

The entire sprawling railway station was struck with gloom and all the rooms were locked from outside. Neither any personnel in blue uniform nor any porter could be seen anywhere. However, the commuters made a madding crowd; they were from every part of the country. It appeared as if they were travelling for the first time. Complete silence prevailed; one could guess that all the mouths were stitched. The traveller wearing a white turban looked around with piercing eyes; his wife held his left hand tightly. The train with all the doors shut lay sleeping close to the platform. The twilight was already covering all, but no electric lights were seen.

The train's departure time had past long ago. One could easily read restiveness, agitation, and fear on each traveller's face. They had surreptitiously purchased their tickets from the wandering black marketing agents and looked askance at each other; when would we reach our destination. They were from remote corners, men, women, children and the aged. The one wearing a white *Goti* stood propped against the concrete lamp-post. He heard, 'They say there will be no more uniformed men in the country, no engine driver, no guard, nor any conductor. Is it good?'

He heard a reply, 'Whether good or bad, we wish the train left without further delay. The journey is long and cumbersome. I feel hungry. Neither any shop nor any vendor is visible!'

'Be quiet. You guys have no patience and feel famished. Your hunger is never satiated.' Somebody in the crowd said it loudly while walking. It was perhaps a new arrangement.

The one wearing the goti, standing propped against the concrete lamp-post looked askance. His wife continued to hold his hand tightly; she appeared scared. A middle-aged man sitting on his trunk near them was watching them keenly. When the scared wife of the goti-wearing man hinted at that ogling person, he arose and told the couple almost in a whisper, 'I am Nuna, I was a railway guard. The stations have been closed and our uniforms were taken away. We were divested of everything!'

'Hunh!' The white goti-wearing person replied.

All of a sudden some robust persons came running to the platform. Each bore a stick in his hand and stood at the doors of the compartments; each compartment had a single door. The train was very long; never had anyone seen such an elongated train before; one could guess that its rear part was merged in the dusk.

The door of the front compartment was opened by the stick-bearing robust man. People thronged in pushing one another, men, women, children and the aged, women wearing *lehangas* who bore their children over their pelvic bones. They were people of all sorts. But the moment the goti-wearing man and his wife entered the compartment, they were flabbergasted. There were neither any seats nor any births. The windows were shut by nailed wooden slabs, and many others were closed by straps of iron.

Standing tightly against each other, all perspired. The children's eyes protruded due to asphyxiation. The elderly as well as the young pushed out their dry tongues. The moment the door of a toilet opened with a creaking sound, the whole compartment was filled with a stinking smell. Some gas emerged and was defused like smoke. The compartment started widening. Its breadth gradually increased to double and then three times. The passengers were terrified. It appeared like a very huge person, as if swollen by the air filled by a bicycle pump, bearing a bulging belly, with stout and thick moustaches. The passengers sat on their trunks, folded beddings, on spread sheets and many on the uncovered floor. The white goti-wearing man, holding his wife's hand, stood against the wall. The women wearing *lehangas* sat at the centre of the crowd.

A few huge lanterns hung from the roof, the light

making the stick-bearing conductor visible to the goti-wearing person; he was sitting on a stool chair inside the door. A man wearing a netted skull cap, red bush shirt, and trousers of blue night-cloth, heavy shoes, and a check cloth under the collar of the shirt appeared. He, with twisted moustaches and infuriated eyes evinced to the crowd with a movement of his head to sit down.

A thin voice came from outside, 'Cucumber! Cucumber!' The famished people stood up to buy, but the men holding the sticks made them sit down. Twelve inch long and robust necks craned out from the doors, and got elongated a long distance from the platform. The cucumber-man had over ten baskets filled with cucumbers and poured them over the people in the compartment. It was left to the luck of each of them to get any. The one with a white braid thought that the green cucumbers were green electric tubes that would burst inside the gullets of the commuters. A smile was visible on his lips, and the stick-bearing conductor fluttered his nostrils when he looked at him.

The whistle blew and the train moved onwards. As soon as the commuters heard the sound of the moving train, they quivered with fright; they had never heard this kind of sound before. It might be that some wheel was broken, or it was not quite rounded, but was six-cornered. The train slanted towards the right as if it was a barge in water.

The sound gradually subsided and then all felt as if the train had got wings, and started soaring like an albatross. The man wearing the white braids smiled and said to himself, 'The albatross might carry all of us as lumps of flesh yonder the mountains to our destination and then devour us, leaving our skeletons behind.'

The conductor directed the women wearing long garments to stand up. They got up anon. By a whirling movement of his body the conductor directed the women to dance. The women took out bells, and danced along with the conductor in a whirling motion in a ring. But the clang of the bells could not be heard by anyone.

The man wearing the white braids uttered a scornful 'Hunh!' as if he was ruminating, and said, 'It is not actually the conductor, but the wheel of the train that whirls round and round.'

And then the dancing too slowed down, the exhausted travellers sat down to have little naps. Only the conductor with wide eyes and the man wearing the white braids stared at the snoozing travellers. The man wearing the white braids stood aside covering his nose with a handkerchief and kept eying him intermittently. The compartment was ruled by silence, but soon the silence, too, broke asunder; the wheels of the train raised a horrific noise again, and then the train stopped.

'Cold cucumbers! Cold cucumbers!!' The vendor's call came from outside.

The man wearing the white braids cast an angry look at the conductor and asked him, 'Where are we?'

The conductor looked at the commuters who were looking at each other's face with eyes devoid of vision and whispered. He then said to the commuters, 'It is not any cucumber vendor, he belongs to the next station. Our throats are fitted with plastic tubes that is why all sound like the cucumber vendor.'

The man wearing the white braids said rather loudly, 'All lies! This is the same station that we left from!' He held his wife by her arm, looked scornfully at the commuters, and then moved towards the door. The conductor stopped him. He smashed his belly and jumped down along with his wife on the platform. He fell on his face. The conductor too jumped out. He might have struck him with his stick, but in the meantime, the train started moving. He swiftly caught hold of the iron rod and kept dangling.

The man wearing the white braids saw him hanging from the rod. He said to his snoozing wife. 'He did not fall. A wheel of the train is broken which rotates on its axis, just like our earth. Nonetheless, it is not a stadium around which the train moves, just like a bullock of the oil-mills; it is but vertigo.'

Holding his wife's hand he got up slowly and then began assessing the hushed night.

Guest for One Night

He reached there in the last hour of the night, and looked up at the sky. Seeing the array of stars, he realised it was the wee hours of dawn as a pleasant breeze had started blowing. However, he did not feel reinvigorated by the fresh breeze. Already rendered lifeless, he could not move his listless limbs.

It was as if he made it to that place with the help of the light emitted by his own teeth – wallowing, wiping his tears, and whimpering repeatedly. Something was bothering him. He thought if a carpenter found a hard knot in the wood while hammering a nail, it might make a fearful sound. The forehead, too, is like a hard knot of wood: it would make a loud clang if a thick nail is hammered into it. Oh my God!

Since he was familiar with the criss-cross of the paths, and knew all the plateaus, canyons, elevations and depths of ridges and their tediousness, he walked the distance like the horse of a cart that manages to tow the cart on familiar paths without light, and finally wearied and exhausted reaches the destination.

The night of the dark fortnight was really very shameless! But after all it was a dark fortnight; the darkness had enveloped every inch of the surroundings; no electric lamp or even an oil lamp could be seen in any direction, neither in the rural nor in the urban areas. All life appeared petrified. Silence prevailed in all directions. Neither any human being nor any other brute form was seen. After all it was curfew.

He himself wondered how he had managed to reach that place and why he was not stopped anywhere because curfew had been imposed. Why did any dog not bite his leg, and strip him naked? Dogs were in multitudes at all cross-roads and in lanes. Why did he not step over any dog that would have bared its teeth at him? Why not even a single jackal was heard howling? Why did he not come across any cop who would utter in a resounding voice 'Halt!' so that the silence broke and they arrested him for violating curfew and banged him with the butts of their rifles? At least a spirit of darkness, carrying a gun or a revolver could have come out from some house, and kidnapped him, if not slayed him there and then. But no obstacle stopped him. He said to himself, 'It is God's divine way, or it might be that God took pity on him for he came as a heart-broken or chilled mourner to hold his another half to his chest and suck up his grief and infuse life into it with his own self.'

He wanted to gulp his grief as one swigs the venom of a snake from a snake-bitten person to save his life. He too, intended to imbibe the poison from *the-other-half* of his self, at least to revive his old life if not give him a new one, as he crossed the mountains to reach there.

Having crossed the mountain he ambled down to the plains. While he walked, he reflected, 'What is he and what am I? It is a matter of only two moulds, but the pain is the same though the moulds are two; the poison percolates inwardly in the same manner.'

When he neared the hem of the mountain, he espied a dozen or two brute-looking stout and robust horses moving amidst the dense forest. He got hamstrung; not that he was scared of death, but he said to himself, 'If they take out life from me, I have to make sure that I reach near *the-other-half* and realise my dream? Otherwise, he might forever bear the pain of poison all alone.'

He felt as if all was overwhelmed by gloom. And when his eyes could see again, he saw one of the same brutes – its chin was long bearing a pointed beard, and his entire body was hirsute, its tail was long like the broom-like tail of a lion. He saw a foot-long pointed and thick horn at its forehead. He almost lost his breath in fear when he uttered --- 'A unicorn!' that shed hail-like tears on seeing him.

He was flabbergasted and forgot his fear of death. When he gazed into the eyes of that 'unicorn', he gave out such a loud scream that resounded in the jungle up to its peak: 'Jamee...la...laa..laaa.... aaa....aaaa!'

He was none other than Jameel, the light of the eyes of his half; he recognised him. The same contours of his face, the same bridge-like high nose, the same big eyes; the 'unicorn' had already recognised him.

'What a changed form you have assumed? Who has misguided you, my son?' Without waiting for his reply, he neared him and embraced his legs. 'Come, I shall accept even this form of yours. Your father might be wallowing in pain from your separation. I too, am on my way to meet him to share some of the pain of his ailment. Come, let's go.'

The unicorn evinced 'No' by moving his head. He turned his head backwards as if to say, 'Look in that direction!'

He looked in the direction. He sensed a hazy movement of the unicorns. He sensed as if Jameel, the unicorn said to him, 'How could I come with you deserting all those unicorns?'

All of them gazed at the city with burning ire. Some of them raised their limbs and tossed them to produce successive resounding sounds like that of canons.

He could not make out anything. He would voluntarily renounce his body there, while weeping made his eyes like dried apricots, but he compromised with the situation. 'I would surely sit beside you, but I am helpless because my grieving-half might be fixedly looking out for me. God wills, I will return soon.'

A little before it was even tide, he started walking again towards the city.

In the wee hours of that evening, he reached the house near the city. To control his breath, he rested a little on the ground, and then calmly tapped the door with one of his fingers; he got no response. After repeating the knock a couple of times with pauses, he heard, almost in a whisper, a female voice saying, 'Who is there?' He lugubriously said in almost the same low voice, 'I am here? I, *the-other-half* of Shafiq Sahab.'

Then he got a reply in a grave voice, 'He has no other-half. You have already splintered us into many fragments. Is there anything yet to be done?'

'No, no. I am Shafiq Sahab's friend. Please open the door. I have just now come from the other side of the mountain.' He explained in a still lower imploring voice.

He heard the woman's voice saying, 'Will you forgive us? He has neither any half, nor any friend. What wrong have we done to you? What is our sin after all? You have deprived us of even wailing.' He almost choked while shedding tears. Thus, he squatted on the step in front of the door. He hung his head, perhaps waiting until morning dawned.

In the meantime, a shadow as thick as that of the trunk of a felled willow appeared before him, he got up. He uttered in a broken voice, 'Who are you?'

A reply equally low came anon, 'Be not frightened for I know you. He recognised your voice while I was sitting at the window. I know well that you are *the-other-half* of Shafiq Sahab. I saw you were always intimate with each other.'

Then they chatted in whispers.

'They do not even open their door. Perhaps they do not recognise my voice.'

'When there is delusion, one is not able to know even one's own self. Now please go, for he is not in.'

'Where is he?' He inquired.

'Move this way, I shall tell you where he is. You might be feeling pain for him. Aren't you? He too, feels pain.'

'I have come to take it away from him,' he said.

'Come. I shall escort you to see him. Are you able to walk? You might be wearied.'

'Those that deprived him of his life are now there to seek his revival.' The unknown person muttered and after heaving a deep sigh, said to him. 'He is still living.'

They walked together and he said, 'There is no other way to keep living.' After a little silence he said, 'Do you know, Jameel is still living, but in the form of a unicorn; I saw him like that.'

'What? Unicorn? I hope you are in your wits. Being shocked is alright, but all have to quaff this potion. I swear by my faith, it is a fact. You see there are so many families like him that got ruined. There is hardly any access to the cremation ground and cemeteries.'

It was not clear why he was not inclined to give his ears to such talk. He tried to divert the chat, 'Strange! Not even the barking of any dog is heard. I wish a dog hovel could be heard!'

'Dogs? There are no dogs left. They were devoured by more dangerous dogs. You know some dogs go rabid.'

'Rabid dogs!' He expressed his astonishment. His companion tried to bring it home to him, saying, 'Barking could easily give a clue to their place, and that would have meant their death. They say that they expended thousands of bullets to silence the barking of the dogs.'

After a little silence he continued, 'Take care. Use a matchstick to light your cigarette.'

Once again he changed the topic, 'Jameel did not die... they thought that they had killed him!'

'You are a simpleton, saying "he did not die", *ha!ha!ha!* A nail of steel was driven into his forehead, a wedge like nail. But by God's grace, the nail proved to be hollow and blood congealed within its cavity; not a single drop was split.'

He screamed on hearing this, but shut his mouth anon, for he was admonished not to give out any loud voice. He would weep in a loud wail, but his pain was ossified within him. He apologised for screaming so loud and then he said to himself, 'Who is a simpleton, you or I? It was a nail of steel that turned into a horn... thick and stout horn ...a pointed one!'

'A pointed horn!' He said. 'Jameel, turned into a unicorn. I espied numerous unicorns of that type at the helm of the mountain while I was crossing over to this side. I am not lying. Yes, I think you are possessed. If the God of Darkness hears you, he might inflict much pain on you.'

Both the wayfarers assumed silence and continued walking onwards. The silence was so intense that he could clearly hear the resounding of his own heart. The silence cracked when low laments of some women were heard; the sound of the rivulet provided the lament with music, it appeared as if nymphs were engaged in lamenting. '*Hushh!* Do not utter any sound!'

'No, I won't. But why do they lament?' He asked him.

'A swarm of hornets sucked their redolent rose, and the white lily-like skeleton was dropped into a cesspool. They are not lamenting, they are feigning a nymphs' song!'

'Now walk over this ridge, but cautiously. The light of day is here and we are about to reach.' His companion told him.

He looked upward, and then to the right and then left. He saw young willows and young poplars dancing in the air or, it might be, they too were lamenting. His heart was moved and he said, 'The trees too are engaged in a nymphs' song?'

'Some spirit has gripped you. I swear to God it is the will-o'-the-wisp that has possessed you!'

He then pondered that there might be some truth in what he said. He had seen such other morning scenes many times in the past. He never thought them to be a delusion!

'Look, the Garden of Paradise is there! He is there inside.' His companion told him.

'Garden of Paradise!' He inquired with surprise.

'It is a garden of new paradise where a stream of milk is soon expected to flow down, and *houris* shall be seen all around. And there to that side, he shall be seated in a big hall. He shall be having the company of a few persons who follow him like his shadow. Do not be frightened, but at the same time have all your senses on alert.'

He started. 'But no plant or tree can be seen there!'

His companion replied, 'Those aged trees have perished, the new scions are being irrigated with milk, and they shall one day show their full verdure.... So, let me leave, for I cannot reveal my face to him. Besides, there is curfew. If we keep living, we might meet again.'

He kept ambling forward and said, 'Listen!' After a second he again said, 'I am saying this to you.'

He looked around, but the plain field was all but ridges and mounds; his guide was not visible. He appeared at a distance, reduced to a dot.

Thus, he said to himself, 'I wonder if he ran away to go back. Is he afraid of light? I did not even see his face, nor did I ask his name.' For a moment he was transfixed but then he made his legs move towards the Garden of Paradise. Lifeless tree-logs stood like grave stones to his left, right, behind, and ahead.

Somehow he managed to reach near the hall at the helm of the plateau. While looking around, he espied his Other Half sitting near a big grilled window and looking out. Near the second window stood four young men gossiping with one another; they wore tidy suits and boots. When they saw him ambling towards the grilled window, their eyes and ears were alert. He tried to evince a smile to his Other Half; he wished to run to him, hold him in a tight hug and weep loudly. Then he would give him Jameel's clue.

He saw his Other Half turning towards him. Without standing up and without greeting him, he said coldly, 'So, you came? I knew you would come. Come in and see the miracle.' He pointed his right arm outwards. He felt stifled when he observed a smile on the lips of his Other Half and he whispered to himself, 'That indicates that he has no information about his son getting metamorphosed into a unicorn.' He sat facing him near the window sill.

His Other Half said smilingly in a very interesting way, 'Look, how high this hall is from the ground, that rounded valley is surrounded by troughs and crests of the plateau! Look there, how the fossils of the erstwhile walnut trees and plane trees look black and shining. Until yesterday I had seen many fossil objects, it takes them millions of years to turn into fossils. Sir, we are ahead of others in all respects, see the advances in science and technology.'

In utter amazement he heard him, while he stared at Shafiq who continued saying to him, 'Both the trees were given some chemical fertiliser that washed them. They used big machines to fill this big abyss with clay. You know the machine that is used to remove snow, a machine like that which is as huge as a house, was used in filling. Perhaps it was like that. Isn't it?' He asked the young men standing there. All the four replied in unison. 'We filled the abyss with our own hands in four days. We washed the trees with chemicals. Afterwards some experts came and used machines to dig out the filling and to test what chemical we had used. They tried their best but failed to get any hint so far.'

His Other Half said, 'Think, getting transformed into a fossil within two years! Look carefully, the leaves are all the same with the same veins, the same branches, the same bark, and the same walnuts. Now look that way! How that canopied plane tree is there with its pretty boles and leaves!'

He looked at him and uttered 'Hmmm'.

Shafiq continued saying, 'If they were still living, sooner or later they would petrify. They say that fossilisation helps to keep them living until the world lasts. Alas! They have closed these lion-like windows with bars. Otherwise, we could use the staircases to go down and be near them, see them, touch them with our hands, and deeply feel their beauty.'

Having heard all this, he reflected; his lips and nostrils started quivering. He thought they have made him such a king as stood naked, but he said to everyone, 'See how pretty my silken dress is!'

He had come to this side of the mountain so he could absorb the poison that had percolated his body, but that venom had already been sucked out. He stood still, as if petrified!

The Other Half stood up and said, 'What strange musings! Walk.'

He strode ahead, like a petrified body, and his Other Half, strode with the hope of good tidings while crooning something. The young men, at a distance of ten to fifteen paces, walked after them, but like spectres.

While pacing forward, he kept mulling over what

all this was. 'May be I am wrong. I came to share his grief, and he is overwhelmed by forgiving! He might be under the influence of some teacher's advice. He was about to burst into weeping, and thought there was no other option. In order to know his mind, he said, 'Do you know... unicorn ...? *Hmmm*?'

'Do you mean that fictitious one-horned species?' The Other Half asked him.

'No, not fictitious, I tell you a fact. I saw them myself... as many as a dozen. I guess they might come down here tomorrow, if not today.'

'Ha...ha...ha! This is your misgiving... Please take care, do not transfer this fear to me, for I am your Other Half.'

'No, it is not my fear, I tell you a fact.' He said again.

'You are telling me a blatant lie. You might have passed some graveyard.' Shafiq said rather peevishly.

He too was in ire, and said with his feet firmly on the ground. 'You think what I say is false, and what you say is true. Whatever you said while sitting there at the window or made a show of it? You called the denuded trees as witnesses and turned into fossils?'

The Other Half continued ambling while dangling his arms, and remained deaf to what he said. After a little reflection he said, 'If you still have the venom of any manner or grief, I am here to absorb that in this frame of myself.'

'Damn! What do I say to you?' He thought his Other Half is not inclined to hear his old sufferings from anyone. About to burst, he wanted to analyse everything thoroughly, 'Then, is Jameel's incident false? Has he not turned into a unicorn?'

He was in rage while giving ear to all this and said aloud, 'What is this hapless idiot!' He raised his head and cast a slap on his face. 'Get lost!' He was in frenzy and started talking nonsense. He tore his clothes, took to running and went away.

He too would have run after him, but four young men somehow changed their dress, chased him, and caught hold of him by his arms. He knew he was caught. All four men had revolvers hanging from their broad belts.

Their senior said almost in a shriek, 'You are Satan. We have almost brought him under control, but you played with his life. Take him!'

He evinced a smile and said, 'Truth cannot be kept under cover for all times, however you may try. Be it a fragrance or an obnoxious smell, it cannot be confined, it diffuses in all directions.'

They took him to the place where a huge wooden mortar could be seen amidst a few cottages. The senior young man climbed over it and sat. To his left stood another young man; the other two kept him in between. It appeared as if he was the Judge and the accused stood at a lower level.

He said, 'You are not judging me alone, but also the other person who escaped.'

'Shut up! Don't you know what court is this?'

'Ha..ha...ha...The one who is an assassin, is the policeman as well as the judge!'

'You mean to contempt us? Do you know what punishment it merits, Satan?' The person standing beside him drew his revolver from the left of his belt, and was about to fire at the target, but the Judge stopped him by putting his arm in front of its barrel, and he put the machine back into his belt.

'Tell me your name,' the Judge asked him.

'A human being!' He replied.

'Hmm. A weird name. There is no such name in our country!'

'This is the name that everyone bears. You alone are name-less.'

'False! Absolute sham! Check his arms.' He ordered.

They drew up the sleeve of his shirt to see and then said, 'Sir, there is something round of green colour and there is a curve to its right end.'

'So, the species is revealed. Imposter!' The Judge passed the sentence, and inquired, 'Which place do you belong to?'

He felt a haze in his eyes and said to himself, 'I don't remember but I think I have seen this person wriggling through a crowd bearing a bundle of tickets in front of the cinema hall, or was he the one wearing heavy nails in his boot climbing up to the gables of his neighbours. Or it may be that I am having these strange premonitions.'

He reflected and then said, 'Of this very land and you? I think you are known to me.'

'Shut up!' The Judge interrupted him loudly. One of them was about to strangle him, but the Judge stopped him.

The Judge questioned him, 'We made you disappear by casting a charm! Why did you reappear?'

He replied, 'I will reply to that question later. For the present, I have come with the intention of sharing the grief of my Other Half.'

'How do you know him?'

'I am the other form of his being. We have grown up together.'

'This will not save you. Tell us since when do you know him.'

'For about six thousand years.' He said.

The Judge guffawed loudly and said to him, 'Are you out of your wits? Or do you have some tacit end in view to say such gibberish?'

Then he ordered his men, 'Take him to that head of boulders, and make him count six thousand.' Then he said to him, 'If you count less or more, you shall have to face the gallows.'

They were about to drive him away, but he pulled back and said, 'I can even count the stars, why just six thousand?'

The Judge took out a cigarette, and the young man standing there lit a matchstick. After a little reflection, he consulted the standing youth, and then passed the judgment.

'We have come to the conclusion that you are here to spy on us and rupture our unity. You are responsible for making Shafiq Sahab tear his clothes by reminding him of Jameel and making him writhe in pain. You are a devil! And you know the end of the devil? You are to get interred while living!' He ordered while getting up, 'Take him near the edge of that small ditch!'

While he walked, he looked at the sky. No flying creature was visible. The Garden of the New Paradise seemed like it was howling. The gales of wind caused that kind of sound.

When he reached the corner, he espied a person tied with ropes to a dead tree. He kept his head hung; he did not raise his head even when they passed him, nor did he show any movement.

'What is his fault? Please set him free.' He pleaded with a pitying face.

'He has already been set free.' All of them said in one voice and untied the rope; the person fell down like a log of elm.

He gave out a shriek and said, 'What answer do you have to all this? Adam was not born in this world for this end! The unicorns are fast advancing and you will not find a chance to escape!'

'Silent! You better think of yourself. Tell us if you have any last wish before you go down this ditch. Let's see if we might be in a position to fulfil that wish.'

He said to them, 'I wish I had hugged Shafiq and died then.'

'He will not come here. You made him flee. You wasted all our toil. We shall soon grant you freedom. Be happy.'

They hammered four pegs into the ridge of the ditch. They got a staircase and made him climb down into the ditch. He was tied with a rope so that he could keep standing; the rope was fastened to the four pegs.

The Judge ordered, 'Now fill up the ditch with those boulders there.'

In no time the ditch was filled up. Then they put earth over it and flattened the surface. All this was seen by Shafiq too, who came running after changing his clothes.

'Oh no! Did you inter my Other Half there? Why did you do so?' He tossed his hand on his forehead, and tears burst forth from his eyes.

'He was a mischief monger, Devil! He had come to collect information.' The chief of the group said.

'No, he was not that type. Or that I scolded him that is why? We two scolded each other many times like that. That hardly matters. Oh God, now that poison is percolating my body.'

They gazed at him. He wiped his tears and turned to the chief young man. 'Will you do me a favour?' He asked him.

'If it is worth doing, and within our power, we may do it.' The chief of the young men said in reply.

'He too, shall be changed into a fossil within two years?' Shafiq said.

'Yes, no doubt about it.' The young man consoled him.

'You may grant that fossil to me.' Shafiq demanded.

'What do you have to do with that?' The chief asked him in amazement.

'I would keep it preserved in my house. I would see it off and on and get solace. Jameel's grief too might get diminished by that.' Shafiq implored with a pitiful look.

'Do you really know what you say? You say what is not right for us to do.' The chief said to him. 'Do you understand me?'

He was dismayed. He moved towards the ridge around the ditch and sat there in the posture of praying.

The chief looked at him, and then at his cohorts. He was in rage, and his eyes shone brightly. In a low voice he said to his cohorts,

'We may not keep that promise! Was that person we buried, right in saying that they are 'one' for the last thousands of years?'

They glanced at the ditch. The chief calmly ordered them, 'You shall empty the ditch tonight!'

Butter-Thief of Jasoda

People thronged around the *Arthi*, stopped and paid obeisance to it when the small funeral procession passed through the markets. The vehicles took to the sides and stood still until the *Arthi* passed; every one heaved long sighs. They did not look towards the *Arthi*, but all eyes were focused at the person who walked alone to lead the *Arthi*.

It was a seven-year-old boy who was attired in a new white *Dhoti* and white cotton sweater. He wore a huge white turban on his head; the shaved head and long hair wisps could be clearly seen through the turban. Seeing this young innocent boy, one could easily guess that the one in the coffin was also someone young who had been summoned from the other world. The people moved and kept chanting:

Raghupati raghav rajaram,
Patita paavan sitaram

The bystanders on both sides also chanted the same, but in a whisper. The boy leading the procession clapped his hands while chanting the line; and kept looking at the bystanders to his left and right. He also looked at the women who craned their heads through the windows of the surrounding houses. But no one evinced even a slight smile on seeing the boy as he expected.

He felt elated for being dressed in new clothes; he was wearing this kind of attire for the first time. He felt his clothes were just like a costume that the 'butter-thief' Krishanji on the calendar wore. While clapping his hands, he also tried to move his legs and feet and tried to wear a smile on his lips. But the sundry people maintained a mournful look and kept looking down and wiping tears from their eyes. This irked him and he reflected, 'If I wore the mask of Lord Krishna, and wore coloured clothes instead of the white ones, all would be cheered. I wish some boy appeared and besmeared my clothes with colours as they do during the festival of *Holi*. People looking at me would surely laugh. As soon as any child showed his head through any window, the mother shoved him away by an elbow kick.

Raghupati raghav rajaram

The procession followed him, but no one appreciated him. In the meantime, he heard the sound of some drums; he was startled. His face showed a red tinge and his legs were about to move in dance.

They reached a crossing of three paths. The bevy

publicising a cinema played the drums and reached quite near. His quivering was just like the *Bhangra* dance. He looked askance to see the drum player, and then looked at his father who was in the funeral procession.

He swerved, walked ahead of the drum-beater, and started his *Bhangra* dance. Someone in the procession said loudly, 'Mercy Oh God!' and then said, 'This portends bad.'

His father chanced to see him. He quickly ran and got him back while holding him by his ear. Tears glistened in his eyes; his attention, nevertheless, was on the drum-beater and he kept casting looks at him and moving his limbs with the rhythm of the drums.

Raghupati raghav rajaram....

The procession kept moving ahead, the drum-beater ran. The sound of the drum came with a gust of air. His legs stopped moving with the drum beat. He felt as if he was meandering and shedding tears. He might have finally felt the death of Jasoda.

His Dream

He started:

Night - a long, dark, frosty, deserted night. There was silence all around. Initially the dogs used to bark and howl up to midnight, but later their howling diminished and finally disappeared. The dogs might have been killed by poisoning or people tamed or fed them to make them silent. Yes, most probably the latter is true because I am not sure when their howling stopped after midnight - or before that. What I know for sure is that the moment they stopped howling, one could sense the smell of roasting meat. Which place did that smell come from? There was no spark or flicker visible neither from the right nor the left side of the cremation ground. Where did that smell of roasted meat come from?

He said, 'I was frightened and peeped through the crevice of the window. I do not remember clearly whether

I peeped through the window opening or hiding in a denuded willow copse behind a thorny bush, I looked out with my shrunken eyes. I wished someone walked the yonder road and talked to me so that the dead parts of my body showed some kind of quivering. I wish there was a rupture in the silence of the night! Ah! Could someone foot over the icy laden road and make the ice produce a cracking sound! Oh, I wish the veil was unbuttoned! But nothing happened.'

I continued musing, and kept watching with wide open eyes. The more the night lengthened, the more I winked and yawned. I did not blink my eyes and kept staring into the sky. I wish a star flickered behind the black clouds! In the meantime, I sighted with my lifeless eyes a long row of black dots coming towards me. Yes, the row of black dots was coming from the direction of the earlier barking of dogs and the smell of roasting meat. The black dots looked like rows roped together by a black thread.

I could sense in the direction of my nose, an infinitely long and narrow tunnel was opened athwart the road. The black dots kept increasing. I got the illusion that they were four legged brutes, all tied to one rope - a weird species, with low shoulders and high rumps. Of course, there are many such animals like horses, cattle, rams, dogs and many others that possess a handsome walking manner; they did not possess that too. They caused sounds of hooves and *chaan-myaan* sounds.

He said, 'As soon as they neared the entry of the

street, I think the first brute tried to trot forward. Its nostrils shuddered with fear and panic. It brayed in its own way. God knows it might have brayed. I saw him getting thrashed by a large stick, but could not see who struck it. Then the brute writhed and wallowed while it was bleeding. It slid down the rime covered street, one after another, many of them, being tied with a single rope. It seemed as if a black train slid through the street. I perceived from some distance that all were like one huge blemish in the deadly narrow alley that finally diminished into one point. I was stunned. There was no moisture in my shrunk eyes.'

He looked at me, and appeared to intimate a message to me.

I said to him, 'You stood half at the precipice, and I gave you company.'

'What of that point…?' he said.

I replied, 'That dot….?'

He did not let me give him a full reply. With his wide open eyes he said, 'The dot? What happened to that dot?'

I said, rather loudly, 'The dot slowly expanded again with the succession tied to the rope. That is, as you say, a black train of brutes, reached the Hasivanj cliff, and then tumbled down into the deep chasm. It struck against the rocks. The silence was shattered. Oh God! Was it a sound or uproar of thunder? Yet Mihagul, who watched the spectacle and guffawed, was stuck like a statue, as if bitten by the darkness. And behind the darkness and clouds was the swerving star. His eyes kept gaping. His long bushy moustaches were frozen like the brooms. If you close your eyes right now and go to Hasivanj, you will see him there half sunk in the earth, in the same posture; his frost does not melt.'

He heaved a sigh and said in a low voice. 'Alas, that interesting dream was smashed into smithereens!'

After hearing this, for some time I felt as if I had sucked out the effect of his tale. But how could I conceal the truth?

I Was Convinced

He said, 'If you do not get irked, I would say all stories are absolutely false.'

My friend said in reply, 'But a falsehood that testifies truth.'

He smiled and said, 'It might be so!'

I perspired for I had met him for the first time. While introducing me, my friend had told him that I wrote short stories. The moment I entered his friend circle, I felt obliged. But later, the issues he discussed with my friend were very interesting, and I scarily got interested in him.

He glanced at my friend and said, 'Yes sir, it might be he is.'

Then he smiled, and said, 'My dear all these stories are lies, and you know, I hate lies.'

Turning to me he said, 'Yes, you might be thinking what a fool I am that I castigate you while being so close to you. Please, do not think like that. Nonetheless, I suggest you have to have courage to be in the circle. I would love your stories. To be candid, many a time lies also entertain us. A Kashmiri has mastery over gossiping.'

Both of them laughed, and I could not abstain. Rather I laughed at his manner of speaking and rolling around his eyeballs.

When he finished speaking, he got serious and calmly said to my friend sitting close to me, 'You know there were two liars'. And when he finished saying, I calmly said to my friend sitting close to me, 'This was said over two hundred years ago by a Latin story writer.'

My friend twitched so I became silent. The other one stared into my face, and then said to my friend, 'Did it feel delighted? What is that book in your hand?'

I handed over the book to him, and he examined it. 'Hmmm! *Rajatarangani* by Orwell! This is what a good book has to be... This is real research. He must have done his research in Kashmir history. However, he was assisted by a Kashmiri scholar'. I told him: 'His steno too was a Kashmiri Pundit. He used to take him along to Sonamarg in summers.'

He said in amazement, 'Really?'

Five days after, we three walked through the market. Two more colleagues met him and they too walked along. Talking about many sundry things, he continued walking, and then suddenly stopped at a place.

'Oh yes, I might tell you something. This is good for research. I was really astonished to hear that RL Stevenson used to come to this place and wrote his stories while camping at Sonamarg. Besides, an interesting thing is that his steno was a Kashmiri Pundit who was named Jiya.'

I felt hamstrung. I lagged behind and moved to the side of the road and stood propped against the wooden grill. My friend gave a boisterous laugh and said loudly to him, 'Why did you make a lie of *even the cotton of Musa*?'

He was irked and said, 'Are you out of your wits? What do you say? My late father told me in those days when he visited Sonamarg, Laddakh, and Kargil.'

My friend squatted on the edge of the footpath. He looked around and found the two colleagues had already left. He strode with long steps and went away.

I went near my friend and made him get up. I said to him, 'I am not angry. In fact I found the one whom I was looking for.'

Yearning

Today, while walking towards the Silk Factory for work, I came across a forlorn white house. There was a strange inkling as I remembered Rajab and those days of Rajab's life when I ran a small grocery shop in his village. It was a dilapidated and tilted shanty erected on four big wooden poles over rounded boulders. Under that shanty was housed my shop and below the shop there was enough space to house all the stray dogs of the village. The shop comprised five to ten cauldrons, mostly empty; and a few contained the rice I got for the things I sold. There were a dozen combs, five to seven soap cakes, tobacco, ropes, hookah pipes, and breads. The porch of the shop was quite big where the children of the village assembled, and raised a din. Rajab, when he was a child, was among them.

Rajab had neither his father nor mother. His mother

had died earlier and when his father died he lived in that village with his maternal aunt. He shuddered when he remembered his father's face. Not that he beat him, but he dragged him to the field for work. He made him break clods, do weeding, keep the landlord's herd of sheep, and do many more chores. Many a time he ran away and sat in my shop's porch for amusement.

One day I asked him, 'What is wrong with you, Rajab that your father always harnesses you and you care a fig for him? It is your good luck that you have him. You have no other kin. Remember, when he is no more, there will be no one to bother about you. Why are you wont to idling?'

He hung his head down, and after a little reflection said in full confidence, 'He is brainless. He wants to keep me busy by keeping the sheep of others. Just a day ago he made me leave school. Look Ismail Kaka, you give me a test and if I pass you please tell him to send me to school. He hardly pays heed to what I say. I promise to do all the household chores and also keep writing on my tablet.'

I espied tear drops glistening on his eye lashes. He looked into my eyes, and then hung his head. All of a sudden he raised his hand and scratched under the few wisps of hair that he had on the front of his head. I said to him, 'Now you leave, I shall tell him today in the evening.'

He felt cheerful, wiped tears from his face and ran away.

In the evening, I somehow persuaded Wahab Magrey, and the next day he sent Rajab to school.

The school was housed over the top of the Revenue Officer's granary. Boys of all the classes studied in that one room. The teacher was a *Moulvi* Sahab with a beard who wore a long black coat, a white turban; he was about fifty years of age. The moment Rajab, carrying his bag under his arm, and a wooden writing tablet in his hand entered the classroom, all the boys laughed loudly. Moulvi Sahab, who sat in a broken chair with his legs on the sill of the window, woke up from his snooze and started. The boys fell silent.

Moulvi Sahab held him by his arm and made him sit among the boys. Rajab looked around. All the boys in the school were from his village, and all knew him well. No one was any stranger. He alone looked like a stranger for his age, his clothes and temple hair. He was a big boy. Rajab's nostrils quivered with anger. He wanted to beat all those boys with his wooden tablet who laughed at him. He contorted his eyes with anger. Moulvi Sahab recognised the boy and said to him, 'You are the monitor of all these boys.'

Whenever Moulvi Sahab was away, or took a nap, Rajab behaved as their senior, kept them silent, and also taught them. He learnt from the boys who were trained, and then taught others. Therefore, Moulvi Sahab was happy with him for he was quick to learn all additions, subtractions, and read many text books, and acquired much knowledge. Moulvi reflected, 'He tasted the thrashing by Moulvi Sahab, and also knew the result of his father's death. Besides, he learnt etiquettes in the house of his maternal aunt. He was adept at picking quarrels with other children, but at the same time he learnt to love others.'

It was a Friday and Moulvi Sahab left to offer mid-day prayers. Rajab engaged himself in helping the boys to solve arithmetic problems. He was teaching them joyfully when he heard the calls – not calls but barking of a dog, 'Rajab! Rajab!' The boys looked out through the windows, only Rajab stood still at his place. The angry call was heard again, 'Rajab, I will come upstairs and break all your ribs. You take me for granted! Will you come down, or should I drag you down?'

Rajab did not reply. His face evinced fear, and his legs quivered. In the meantime, a spruce like tall man came upstairs and slapped him repeatedly, and verily dragged him down the stairs. If there was not some other person accompanying him, he would have been smeared by blood dots. Having brought him down, he asked him, 'Didn't I tell you in the morning not to go to school? You ignored my warning. You bullock of a yokel! Won't you let us live peacefully? You seek prosperity? Utter something. Did your father pay us anything for looking after you? Others might think that is why we bother so much about you.'

Just then Moulvi Sahab arrived. Seeing him, Rajab ejaculated a weeping cry. He felt as if he was a ram ready to be slaughtered on a log. He had a glimmering of hope that God sent Moulvi Sahab to his rescue; as if he was his own father. 'Oh my father!' He bawled. The Moulvi was angry and called him a couple of slangs, that too in Arabic accent. He freed him from the grip. 'Shall I hand you over to the police that you entered the school without permission? Ask the watchman to come here as he tortures a child.'

At first Rajab's maternal uncle was surprised, but when the Moulvi's wrath abated, he took him aside and said, 'The issue is that only the day before yesterday he has hit Sharief Sahab's son and has given him a deep gash. I had to face the brunt. I am living calmly away from even the angels, but he is bent upon getting me excommunicated from the village.'

The Moulvi held him by his ears, and keeping his eyes shut, he said, '*Astagfirullah*! (God forgive us). Then go and strip his skin. I did not know it. Even Sharief Sahab's good son did not make any mention of this event. Now it is okay, I shall ask him now.'

The Moulvi looked up; the boys were craning their necks through the window. Leaving his talk unfinished, he cried to them, 'Why don't you sit away from the window? Wait I shall try my stick on you.' And thus he got himself relieved from the angry man and went up the stairs to his school. In his disappointment Rajab kept watching him until he reached upstairs. Tears trickled down his cheeks, and continued flowing until he was home. He rested his head in the lap of his maternal aunt and was soon in deep sleep.

The next day he ran from his home and reached the porch of my shop. With his head bowed down, he kept standing. Soon he felt restless and was about to leave.

'Rajab!' I called him.

With his back to me, he stood motionless. It was after a couple of my calls that he turned to me, but still with his head hung. 'You have not committed any crime for boys usually quarrel with one another. Do not be scared.'

He said in reply, 'Yes sir, I know you behaved as my good father yesterday when he was about to slit my throat! Sir, I shall not stay at my aunt's house. No one is there to have a word with me except my aunt.'

One day he saw the Moulvi, and he ignored him and walked away. The Moulvi called him, 'Rajab! Why are you being nonchalant and not even greeting me?'

Rajab wished him, but with a grudge.

The Moulvi said to him, 'I had a scuffle with Sharief Sahab only for you. If your uncle too could have a word with him, I could find a supporter.'

Rajab felt happy, and the Moulvi started a new issue, 'If you chance to meet Jamal of Satar the Stammerer, tell him that Moulvi Sahab waited for him. Otherwise, they shall start cleaning. Do you hear? Inform me later.'

Rajab turned back and reflected that it would be better to tell this to his maternal uncle, but he feared that he might thrash him. He mused for a while and said to himself, 'Why not tell my uncle to send a cockerel for Moulvi Sahab so that he allows me to enter the school. But he was terrified that in reply he would get a thrashing instead of giving him the cockerel. After a little reflection, he went running, got a few grains of maize from his neighbour's house and a needle and thread from some other neighbour. There was a ditch behind the potter's shanty and cocks and hens were busy in scratching clay there. While walking to the spot, he threaded the grains of maize which he flung towards the horde of hens and cocks. One of the roosters gulped the maize. He pulled the thread and calmly took the rooster under his garment, and reached the backyard of the school. He remained there until the boys left.

He kept asking himself if he had committed any sin. His mind was buzzing with questions: two and two make four, two into two are four, but what four? Four cockerel or four thieves - four horse thieves – four mischief mongers? But the thieves and offenders are hunted by the police? Am I a thief? What should I do now? While he was musing, Moulvi Sahab climbed down the stairs of the school. Rajab neared him from behind and said, "Moulvi Sahab, I have something to tell you. My maternal uncle sent this winged thing for you. He asks you to do something for yourself.'

As soon as Moulvi Sahab saw the cockerel, he cast a big slap on his face. Then he cursed him saying, 'Did you mean to swindle the Moulvi! How did you get this cock from our coop? Oh God, What has happened to this world? See how evil and unabashed he is! What?' Rajab closed his fist and took to his heels. He could hardly find a moment to think whether to go to Aunt's place or not, and came to my place.

'Aren't you going to your Aunt's place?'

'Is that right, you halfwit?'

'I shall stay in my own hut. And in the night hours I shall...' He could not complete the sentence.

'Where shall you stay during night time?'

'I shall stay over the granary with you. Where else? Do not think that I am afraid at my own home, but...' I was dumbstruck and did not reply.

In the meantime, a group of school children had gathered on the porch. Some of them got busy in scribbling on the wooden tablets and others in solving questions.

'Look, they did not do their homework at their homes and now they are doing it here.' Saying this to himself, he sat near them as if nothing had happened yesterday and he had not quarrelled with anyone.

'Did you not attend school, Rajab?' A boy asked him while hurrying to finish writing the table.

Rajab sighed, and without answering, he said to him, 'Let me help you.'

'Help me in solving this question please, Rajab.'

'It is not a hard question, provided you know complex multiplications, or when you know simple addition. You do not know it. Tell me what is two plus two?'

'Do not try to test me.' Rajab again found himself to be a stranger, as if no one knew him and he knew no one there. As if he was a stranger in the whole village. He did not carry his wooden tablet or he would have surely hurled it at their heads.

For a few days he continued to ingratiate with the boys by saying, 'Will you do this problem? Can you tell me the meaning of that word?' But how long could he continue like that? For a couple of days he could, but after ten days he was again estranged from them. One and one make eleven, but if you say what is true… He had a yearning for education, and this deep longing made him spell out writings on the tobacco wrapping paper. Or many a time, he drew lines on the walls with pieces of charcoal or did additions, subtractions and multiplications. Since he was frightened, he soon wiped all the markings. He felt his heart would burst.

The Palace of the Mute

Well before the break of dawn, the maestro pipers had assembled and started playing *Ragas* in the black marble pavilion of the sprawling garden of the royal palace; thus they woke the kingly inmates of the city from their intimate dreams. Their predecessors had been pursuing this vocation for many generations, and with finesse they played mesmerising tunes to exhibit their art. When delighted, the kings accorded robes of honour to them, besides gifting pearl necklaces, arm-bands and other precious things. The morning melody of piping made their beautiful earth awash with the deeds of love and made their days smiling and blossoming.

Even today, the mellifluous melody of the pipes filled the atmosphere with redolence, but the new king continued changing sides on his divan, with his face gripped with annoyance. He passed many nights in restlessness; even the love-making of the queen did not awaken his latent passions. He perceived the charming melody of pipes as nothing but noise. He plugged his ears with his fingertips, but somehow the melody still percolated in. He lost his temper and pressed a button fitted in the side of his divan. The security guards on duty outside his bedroom sent the personal attendant to the door of the king.

'Long live the king! What should this servant of yours do to cheer you up?'

The attendant said in submission with his head bowed, so that the king did not espy his face so early in the morning.

'Send the pipers away. I have been harassed by the same noise since I assumed kingship; they do not let me have even a little calm. Send a message to the ministers to arrange for a session of the court, but now, without any delay, go anon!'

'The order shall be complied with, my Lord.' Saying this, the attendant left and conveyed the king's message to the security officer. He in his turn, communicated the message to his senior, and the latter conveyed it to the Prime Minister who lifted the phone and sent the message to all other ministers. All of them grew agitated. Their faces hung down heavily, their tongues stammered saying that something bad is in the offing.

In the meantime, the melody of the pipes had stopped as if the arch of the pavilion had caved in over the pipers. However, the warbling of the doves and orioles started welcoming the shining of the mountain cliffs. The king with his eyes shut, clattered his teeth, and was as restive as a live eel in a hot pan. He said to himself, 'All this is nothing but sycophancy — be it the melody of pipes or the warble of the birds. They pose sweetness of affection, but I am sure tomorrow they shall raise a furore so loud that the membrane of the ears might rupture. There shall be a din of doomsday outside my court – we hate noise. I must silence it now. Since I assumed my kingship, the noise has been coming from all directions. The noise is more venomous than a snake-bite in shameless nights.' Then he ejaculated: 'Stop the noise!'

Hearing the harsh cry, the attendant, with his face hidden in his two hands, came in and said, 'What pleases my Lord?'

'Who called you in?'

'My Lord, I heard your loud cry which I am here to obey.' The attendant quivered with fright.

The king said in low voice, 'Did I scream? Do we raise noise over ourselves? Hmmm... You leave. The noise will be interred and mixed with dust.'

The attendant left and reported all this to the security officer who reported all to the prime minister. The prime minister was frightened; he lifted the phone and said in utter amazement and very hesitantly to all his ministers. All grew fidgety, and feared that this portended bad.

While this issue reached the ears of the officers and the ministers, the king hastily covered his body with a silk gown and silken trousers, and moving crawlingly, entered the bathroom. After having a bath, he came out swinging his arms to express his anger. Soon, without reflecting, he entered his sleeping room and holding his hands together, sat on the sofa. He had never done this act before. Normally, he would go to his dining room after finishing his duty in the prayer-room, but today he entered his sleeping room. His personal attendant secretly communicated all these weird actions of the king to the queen, but at the same time he begged for pardon. The queen was nonplussed and decided that the chef should take the breakfast to the king's bedroom and that she too would follow him.

The king busied himself in moving his hand on the soft velvet of the sofa, and assessing all the objects placed in the room including a human-size painting of his father. Then he fixed his gaze on his mother's statue and said to himself, 'All this riffraff belongs to the old-fashioned palace, where every item represents the antiquated thinking of the past kings. The broom-like moustaches are not liked in modern times. All these ministers and attendants are also of primitive fashion. We are already at the threshold of the twenty-first century after kicking aside the twentieth century. Let us tell them, "You know that noise is death for the environment. Your death hardly makes any difference, but if the environment dies, we cannot survive. But will they be able to understand this? Will they?"'

The chef along with two attendants entered. They carried a huge silver tray in which the dishes were contained in gold plates. 'Long live the King!' All three said in unison. Then they placed the tray on the centre table. The king groaned, 'Take all this away. I do not want to eat anything.'

The moment he uttered the last words of his grunt, the queen entered the room. 'May His Excellency accept my greetings! Are you keeping well?' She quietly cued to the chef and his helpers to leave. They left calmly. While nestling close to the king, the queen said, 'Do you grant me permission to sit close to you?'

'What makes you seek permission? A king and his queen are one soul with two frames, or two sides of the same gold coin.'

'What does my Lord want to say?' The queen said while bringing the plates with dainties in front of her master, 'If that were the case, I would have been the charm of this sleeping room and the royal bed. Now please have the food.'

'I don't feel in the mood to eat anything. My nights are ruined because of my restlessness. I hate noise as it deprives man of his sleep. That is the reason I never gave you the trouble of coming to my sleeping room. If God is in our favour, all will set right very soon.' Thus, the king consoled his queen.

The queen replied, 'What is so difficult about stopping the noise? Issue a proclamation to stop the noise.'

The king evinced a slight smile and said, 'It is not so easy. The noise is not just of one kind, it has many faces - the cow's balk too is a sort of noise, the sheep's *myaan* is noise, singing, frolicking, laughing boisterously - all are various sorts of noises. Ha-ha-ha I have already ordered for an immediate session of the court to discuss this issue.'

Nodding in agreement, the queen said, 'That is fine. Let's see what the ministers suggest. For the present please have your breakfast. In case you do not have it, I too shall not have even a sip of water.'

The king fell silent and looked smilingly at his queen's face. She came very close to him and held him fast to her by putting her arm around his waist; they exchanged looks as if Mainka was trying to seduce Vishwamitra. She whispered to him, 'Lord, what is the charm of a kingdom, if we have no scion of our own? Having a prince is a dignity for a king. And then we are a woman and a man, or the queen and the king, why don't we love each other to our full consummation?'

The king held her in embrace, and after kissing and caressing her, he consoled her. 'I am fully conscious of the fact that there is perhaps a hard stone instead of a heart in my body. We are a little late in making love, not by choice, but because of various complications of kingship which did not let me have time for that. You may grace this divan from tomorrow. Is it okay?' He finally gave her a kiss and started having his breakfast.

The court was held, and all the ministers were seated in a disciplined manner in accordance to the hierarchy. All of them were restive, as if seated on chairs of thorns; all kept their heads bowed waiting to hear the king. Silently, the king looked at them one by one as if assessing their hidden motives. When the prime minister did not start the proceedings, the king said loudly almost as if shouting, 'prime minister, why do all of you look so bashful. I think I was expected to be abashed for I know that gems like you are in my court and I stand nowhere in comparison to the shine of the gems. *Ha-ha-ha.*'

While keeping his head bowed, the prime minister said in a meek voice, 'My Lord, we are really ashamed. We beseech you to not humiliate us.'

The king said in ire, 'Then why this silence? You know we despise silence in the court as much as we despise the noise outside that makes us restive. I remember, all the members in the assembly chattered like pigeons in the last meeting. But why are we all so stubbornly reticent today? We do not like that the cooing of our ministers falls silent. On the contrary, I wish that your noise drowns the outside noise. Silence is essential for improving the environment. Noise is the death of environment, and eventually our death, your death. Do you understand?'

The prime minister evinced a nod in affirmation. He stood up and said, 'Lord, every word is absolutely correct. Noise generates problems, while silence buries the problems forever.'

The king hastened to say, 'Then why is it that our council of ministers did not make any advance towards achieving that goal? The council of ministers is a horse that waits for the spur to move; it does not need whipping. For long we have been craving for sleep - there is noise in the daytime and noise during the nights. Outside the precincts of the palace I hear either the lamenting of the people, or the dogs' howling, barking and fighting. At times I also hear the distant cries of people, the beating of drums, Long live! Down with! Does it become a cultured society to raise such noises? If I happened to be a king in the previous century, it was possible that I too would have been habitual of noise. I might have made noise as a component of my nature by participating in various wars. But that is not possible now. We have kicked away the twentieth century to enter the twenty-first century. Science and technology is now an integral part of our life. Noise must end. The rule of silence must be established.'

The prime minister again moved his head in agreement and then he mustered a little courage to say, 'My Lord, if I have your permission, I might narrate an anecdote that might facilitate our efforts to control noise.' The king granted him permission. 'You may narrate the anecdote, our prime minister, but as briefly as possible. Squandering time in our era amounts to reversing the movement of a clock.'

The prime minister stood up and said, 'Sir, it is said that King Akbar once experimented. They say he built a huge palace that was run by deaf and dumb people, whether men or women. This palace was named *Gunga Mahal* (Deaf Palace). The moment a child was born and the mother died during the delivery of the child, or the parents were not in a position to bring up their child, they admitted the child to the Gunga Mahal. Thus, the palace was crowded with hundreds of babies, come from distant areas. It was decreed by the king that no one should enter that palace except the employees who, as a rule, had to be deaf and dumb. When after two years the king got the babies out of the palace, all of them were found to be deaf and dumb. Thus, a legion of such children was produced. It was a very good experiment indeed.'

The king interrupted him, saying, 'He had his own whims. You have indeed developed dotage. How can an experiment like that succeed in our hurly burly times and want of leisure. Will it not take my entire life in getting such thousands of children for the experiment? And then are we to slay all their parents? Why don't you think before you talk? Tell me how many years have I been holding this kingship. Did you even bother to understand my heart in all these years? This is really a regrettable thing.'

The deputy prime minister said anon, 'My Lord, why can't we issue a proclamation to prohibit all manner of noise like laughing, frolicking, singing, dancing, wailing, sloganeering and other forms? Why not ban all types of activities except the lectures of teachers in schools, colleges, and universities? We can fix the routes of all vehicles, trains, and motorcars, and put strict ban on horns. At the same time, we may perish all the horses, cattle, donkeys, dogs and other animals. So far as milk is concerned, we can import it from other countries.'

'Hmmm!' The king evinced almost half approval to this suggestion. The queen suggested mere proscription, but that might not solve the problem. This is the difference in the ways of thinking! Hmmm!

All other ministers in the council hung their heads, but the fifth minister alone stared at the king's face; he was younger in age as compared to others. The king said to him, 'What is your counsel?'

While continuing to gaze at the king's face, the minister said, 'My Lord, noise is of various kinds, and no noise can be stopped as long as this world is there. The noise caused by science and technology, noise inherent in the nature of living things, and thirdly, there is a kind of noise caused by ministers like me and the government itself. What type of noise can we end? Water keeps flowing however we may try to barricade it as it percolates under the heaps of husk. Noise trickles in through crevices however hard we may keep our ears plugged with cotton or sit in noise-proof rooms, though it is not always possible. Noise ultimately gets wearied, and if it does not get exhausted, we should try to know the reason and then eliminate it.'

The king sharpened his eyes with rage, 'Oh, we did not expect this from you. Do we create noise? Do you mean we are hostile to living species? You say noise is inherent in their very nature! Ha-ha-ha! Why did you feel shame in saying that it is their habit? I think arranging today's meeting of the council did not yield any results. I shall now myself, try to seek some remedy. But you ministers say noise is noise! How multitudinous it might be in kind, we shall not let noise annoy us.'

Gasping with wrath, the king stood up and ambled towards his resting room. The ministers started debating with one another. The prime minister and the deputy prime minister caught hold of the last speaker in the council and thrashed him to their full. They were agitated. Their faces were swollen with anxiety, their tongues stammered, for they apprehended something very bad was about to happen. Thus, they held consultations and finally agreed upon summoning all the officers of the country, and order them to stop the noise somehow or the other. All the cattle, other livestock could be driven to the frontiers of the country and arrangements for their shelter may be made there. They thought that such measures might assuage the king to some extent. In case this arrangement succeeds, our esteem will remain and the king's restlessness could be cured.

The king made his personal agents get two reputed scientists in electronics and computer science to his court and had a discussion with them on the issue. Among other things there was a mention of Akbar's Gunga Mahal as well. It was secretly decided that if all those scientists helped the king in silencing noise, they would be rewarded with many riches.

'I beseech you, my Lord that this agreement should not be made public, as our kith and kin might face trouble.' One of the scientists said.

The king told them confidentially that they should remain without anxiety and give up their apprehensions. 'Is there a king who does not keep his promise?' He said.

The two scientists went to a corner and had a conversation. After a little while they came back, and one of them said to the king, 'Our Lord, we are sure to finish noise.' The other scientist looked around, as if he sensed that somebody was eavesdropping with his ears clasped to the wall; he whispered something to the king.

The king felt delighted and said, 'That is what I want. It is the tongue that makes or mars one.'

The first scientist reflected a little and said to the king, 'It needs a little construction work. The earlier we complete that task, the easier it would be to fulfil your desire.'

The king said eagerly, 'How large is the work that you talk of?'

The second scientist said, 'Sir, the work could be completed in two days and even in two weeks. Actually, there is nothing complex about it: we have to raise a structure resembling the shed of some factory with a wide door to enter and a door to exit. From the exit door, there has to be over a three miles long and wide path covered with iron sheets on both sides. That is all.'

'This task can be finished in four days,' said the king.

'Sir, we shall return to see you on the fourth day after the beginning of the task, and then discuss other details of the program.'

'You may come in your personal vehicles and in disguise.' The king said to them.

The two scientists left after seeking the king's permission and the king entered his sleeping room; he was very happy. He anon called his queen, but made no mention of his plan.

'Our Lord may accept our salutation.' Saying this, the queen entered the sleeping room. 'You look much spirited today. What orders are there for me to obey?'

'What? You and my orders! Are you different from me? How can I order my own self? Ha-ha-ha…' The king said, placing his hand over the queen's hand.

'Is there any special reason for this reminder?' the queen asked him.

'We want to fulfil our promise. From today onwards, when we finish dinner in the dining room you shall come to grace the bedroom beside me.' The king said to her.

'The order shall be complied with.' The queen replied.

'Words like *order* and *compliance* do not mean anything in matters of love; only desire and flame of love matter in this sphere.' The king said in a voice that expressed compassion.

Four days elapsed, and the two scientists appeared in the evening. They found the king rather morose. Showing caution, they inquired the reason. The king told them that the task was still half finished. 'We have dismissed many engineers for the delay. You shall have to wait for a couple of days more.'

The scientists also felt perplexed. On hearing about the dismissal of the engineers, their anxiety increased as they feared their own dismissal. They stood with their heads bowed.

'Do not be worried. In case they delay beyond three days, they are sure to be beheaded.'

Without raising their heads they quivered in fear. The king observed this and said, 'You please sit at ease. I think you are feeling the chill.'

'Our Lord, it is not the cold that makes us shiver; we felt the chill on hearing the mention of the heads.' One of the scientists said while continuing to hang his head.

'But why?' The king asked in an authoritative tone.

Fearfully, the second scientist said in a broken sentence, evincing a smile but with numb lips, 'Your Excellency! Ha-ha-ha., how to say it? I mean this that… ha-ha-ha, we… we did not have…. I mean… the day before yesterday… in haste… there is one thing that… we forgot… Your Excellency…'

Both of them got up and then lay down at the king's feet. The king was amazed, and said 'What did you forget? Tell me in plain words. Do not prevaricate.'

'We beseech you to save our lives, Your Highness! Our heads ... your Highness…are precious to us, yet we are ready to remain at the mercy of the lotus like feet of your Excellency. Have mercy on us…your Excellency… Ha-ha-ha.'

The second scientist was quick to say, 'Your Excellency, We forgot to say that the city has to be covered all around with barbed wire so that people do not move in and out without seeking permission. Our carelessness might cause some more delay.'

'That means there are hurdles!' The king said rather angrily. 'You mean we shall have to pass more days in restlessness. *Hunh*!'

'Your Excellency! Have mercy on our lives. Our heads are at your disposal, but we wish that they be not severed from our bodies.'

The king inquired in a grave tone, 'Do you think it would take much time?'

'Your Excellency! If the work is started today, and from all the four sides, then it would not take much time. We mean, Your Excellency, a week or ten days at the most.' The first scientist said while clenching his teeth.

'You forgot this important task of the project! I am amazed.' The king expressed his displeasure.

'That is why we are remorseful. That is why, Your Excellency we are… I mean… supplicating for exemption from beheading.' With folded hands the two scientists appealed to the king.

'Is there any other aspect of the project that you have missed? This is the time to say.' The king asked.

'Your Excellency, this was the only issue that skipped our attention. The human brain, Your Excellency, many a time is overwhelmed by forgetfulness.' The two scientists said.

The king said to them, 'Now you may leave, but be sure that you come here on the evening of the ninth day, at the same time and start your work. All shall be ready by then.'

The two scientists were joyous for being spared from beheading and both left moving backwards and bowing in saluting.

When the two scientists were gone, the king said to

the prime minister, 'Before the scientists complete their work, we shall proclaim throughout the entire city that our subjects maintain silence while they remain engaged in their work. Tell them that I, their king, abhor noise because noise disturbs our mind, and makes our brain ache which then affects our entire body. Prime minister, you might agree with me that the rule of a king depends mainly on his ability to curb all manner of noise in his kingdom.'

The prime minister nodded his head in agreement. The moment the king finished what he had to say, the prime minister said while raising his folded hands, 'Your Excellency, the task will be accomplished by today evening. Now tell us, if there is any other command for us.'

'Direct the people that sorrow has to be contained in their hearts. Only those people wail who do not feel their sorrow pervaded in their innermost. If the king per chance hears any lament or laughter from people in frenzy of joy, their attempt to shatter the tranquil demeanour of the king shall not be ignored. On the contrary, he might tie them to boulders and throw them into the river. The king shall strip their bodies of their skin while they live.'

Saying all this, the king stood up in rage. The prime minister's legs shook with fear. He could hardly make his voice say, 'Whatever pleases His Excellency.' Having said this, the prime minister left the royal palace. The king felt pacified and in a joyous mood he entered his private chamber where his queen was waiting for him. When he entered the chamber, all of a sudden he had a fit of rage again as he found all the doors and windows of the chamber open and all the noise of the hustle and bustle of the city flowed in. He cried angrily, 'Close all the doors and windows so no noise finds a way to enter the chamber.'

All the maids and attendants ran to shut the windows and doors tightly; the noise subsided. In the meantime, the far off sound of drum beats announcing scavenger could be heard. Hearing it, the king felt happy and said to the queen. 'From now onwards all the citizens of the city shall feel suffocated and rendered deaf and dumb'. The queen put her plump arms, softer than butter, around the king and held him tight to her bulging chest.

The maids and female attendants continued jingling the bells of their anklets while the king and the queen had their union.

The scientists started fencing the borders with barbed wire. The plebs were amazed to watch this and gossiped. Nevertheless, no one dared to ask what this barbed wire fencing meant. Ultimately, someone leaked the secret and people came to know about the real issue. This happened when about three-fourth of the borders were already fenced. After that the citizens consulted their elders and resolved that before the entire border was sealed with barbed wire, they should in small groups stealthily escape in the dark of the night.

When after some time the king came to know that the scientists have accomplished their task and the entire city has been completely fenced, the king was in ecstasy.

He climbed up to the gables of the highest balcony; all was still and silent. The king relaxed and called for the prime minister, who appeared in a little while. Joyously, the king said to him,

'We are very happy with you, prime minister. The task of imposing silence on the city that we entrusted on you has been accomplished with complete success. Tomorrow the time is propitious. Let it be proclaimed in the city that all our subjects gather in the central park so that we confer robes and awards to the scientists, and thus complete the auspicious project.

The prime minister cast a glance at the king and said, 'We might look for the subjects, but where? I made a visit to the city today early in the morning. The entire city is absolutely emptied of people; all have fled along with their belongings. Even the jackals have stopped howling.'

'What? What do you mean?' asked the king in anger.

Saying this, the king got up. 'Get the scientists here. We shall get them stripped of their skin while they are alive. If all the borders were properly fenced how could the people escape?'

The prime minister said to him, 'Your Excellency, who shall we rule now? Shall we rule the deserted city or the dried up fields?'

The king replied, 'No, no. We shall go and drag all the bullocks back.'

In the meantime, a clamour like that of the Doomsday was heard from outside. The king was stupefied.

'Look, they are there. How could they survive without

us? See, they have returned.' Saying this, the king went up to the balcony and looked out at the ground. The entire city had assembled, but outside the fence of the barbed wire. Together they pulled down the fence and advanced towards the royal palace. Seeing this spectacle, the king swooned and fell down from the window of the highest balcony. The crowd watched him falling and ran towards the carcass of the king. And then there was tumult of victory. The sweet melody of the drums and reed-pipes filled the air and the entire city was in rapture.

Story of a Painting

Asha could find no rest. She would walk in the room and then sit, while leaning her body against the wall, or let herself fall on the cushioned bed. She felt an urge to cry loudly and weep, and lament over her destiny. But a faint glimmer of hope in some dark recess of her heart stopped her from doing so. Thus she writhed like a fish without water and sobbed, and then rays of hope brightened her eyes which soon dimmed and gloom filled them. Some unknown gloom made her restless. The state of her despondence was such that it did not let her have any moment of solace. Her husband had ruined all her aspirations. His indifference to her had reached the limits and break-up of the nuptial tie seemed imminent.

In the state of pangs, the memories of old days came one after another to her mind. She felt herself whirling like a spin top the stopping of which could not be predicted.

When she was in college, she sneered at her girl-friends. She called them stupid. 'How long shall you continue playing with dolls?' Then she grew serious and reflected, 'No, Oh me! One must not get betrayed in love. Love is no love if it is short-lived. And love does not last forever. If it continues, it lasts hardly up to marriage; then it collapses and breathes its last. The moment a lover's funeral takes place the beloved starts a new game of marriage.' She often made her friends understand this enigma of love: 'Love before marriage is a bush that does not flourish into a tree. Love is nothing but the rising and ebbing of emotions. If you do not get your love, you suffer separation. And if you get it, you have to keep weeping and fear separation. If destiny is in your favour, your love gets consummated into marriage. ...But all the pleasures end.'

Asha believed that a girl must love her husband, and that love is strengthened by the nuptial tie. Why should one blindly agree to a marriage arranged by one's parents? A boy too, should first spend enough time to understand the girl who is going to be his spouse. Only then the kites of love fly smoothly and the threads do not break easily. Only then the kites reach the moon, if not the Sun.

After completing her education, Asha desired such a world of dreams. She was married to Mr L who was a professor of economics in a college. Soon after marriage the ocean of love swelled into tides. The ocean was so wide and deep, that it was not possible to fathom it. And why not? In her youth, she had stopped the streams of emotions from making the ocean swell into a deluge.

She had controlled her desires and the swaying yearnings from raising their heads like a snake-keeper does not let the snake raise its head out of the container, and keeps the brute curbed in the container for days and months. When this image appeared in the eyes of Asha, she felt a pang of sorrow. 'Oh! I could keep the lid of the container open.' She ruminated. 'I wish the snakes of my desires and cravings bit me once and for all as had happened with some of my girlfriends.' She heaved a long sigh in despondence.

Just a few days after her marriage with Mr L, she wanted to express her longings to her spouse. But Prof L was busy in preparing class notes from books and uttered '*Hunh*' and '*hanh*' to evade the topic. Asha thought it was not nice to disturb him when he was so busy. She cheerfully moved from one room to another of her new house as if she was a *Mynah,* flying and warbling at will. Her time no longer belonged only to her, but to her spouse as well; eventually his world was her world. All seemed to suggest that the violin of her love was readily available; it was just a matter of removing the cover and striking the chords. Once the chords were struck, Asha was ready to dance for her husband. A couple of days passed, but the chords were not struck, nor did she dance. Prof L was busy even in the evening, but Asha ventured to chat. The pen in Prof L's hand was ready to slip therefore, he evinced a deaf smile and said, 'You talk something foolish.' Asha, in all compassion said, 'Do you call it unwise? It is the lamp that dispels the gloom over this colourful world. Love is always averse to darkness, isn't it?'

Her husband said rashly, 'It might be. But tell me what new lyre are you carrying today?'

Asha, overwhelmed by passions said, 'It is this new lyre that resolves all the problems of life. The moon, the stars and the whole universe envy us for having it.'

Prof L could not control himself. He gave a huge laugh and said, 'Very good! Excellent! I did not know that you are good in poetry also.'

Asha felt modest and said, 'I am no poet, but all the environs of nature urge us to be steeped in such spectacles. The moon… the stars…'

The Professor said without reservations, 'The moon, the stars, nature - Why do you praise them? Human beings are supreme among all and have brought all of them under his control, and is almost ready to harness them to his benefit? You are there to use them as toys of your passions!'

Asha interrupted him saying, 'Now will you get up or not? Let's go outdoors. Look there, the moon shines in the sky. Let us see what spectacles the air has in its store. This is the real time to get absorbed and lost in each other.'

The Professor laughed and said, 'I knew that people said love needs to be revealed, but I thought that was before one's marriage, but I had neither heard nor seen such a condition of anyone after marriage.'

'You shall surely feel the same condition yourself.' Asha replied. 'The urges of love are like that.'

Professor L stared at her in amazement. 'I fail to understand what you want. All granted, but I never knew that men and women love one another in the same way as they did before marriage. No, it is not possible for me that we meet each other in the streets and alleys instead of our private rooms. Or be always on guard to escape people's detection as if we were crazy lovers. I cannot even afford to ask you to be huff for a few days and not enter my chamber, so that I might write a song on separation, or send you a love-letter, or catch hold of you on the stairs, avoiding the servant's looks, hug you there, and shed tears of pity.'

Asha said in vexation, 'What then? You don't love me?'

'Not the way you want,' the Professor said. 'That is a meaningless way, quite artificial. May be one does it before getting married; but after marriage...? You think about it yourself...Now we have to shoulder responsibilities. We have to care about our family.'

Interrupting him, Asha said, 'All such responsibilities keep arising, yet love has its own ways. You strive to earn a name by making basic changes in the principles of economics, you may earn it, yet you cannot attain immortal fame. Love, on the contrary, is eternal; it helps man become immortal.'

In order to end the arguments, the Professor took a book in his hand and got absorbed in it; Asha had to leave in a sad mood. All her hopes got swept away and turned into dust. Pondering over this incident, she felt weakened. She kept changing sides on her bed and sobbing; after all, it was a question of her life. Having reached a cross-road, she was not able to decide which way to go. She still believed that all her girl-friends had ruined their lives by following the routine path. Nevertheless, she had a glimmer of hope that she still had time to decide her own way. Even then a thin and unintelligible line was carved in her mind. 'Why not separate from such a husband who is not familiar with the word 'love'? How can my life attain its fruitfulness with such a husband? I wasted my life until marriage. How can I fulfil all my cravings and yearnings after my marriage? It is not possible to spend my life with a dry-tempered professor. Why not remarry so that my love begets love?' Engrossed in such musings, she again lay down on her bed. She wept and moaned. A flow of memories flashed in her mind that led her to envision a picture, the picture of Prakash. This was the sole image that dispelled her gloom and anchored some hope in her. She started execrating her own self. 'I wish I had showed my inclinations towards him when he had stretched his hand to express his love for me! I would have been free from this nuisance by now.' She cried again.

Months after her marriage she had somehow persuaded her husband for an outing though he was not ready to waste his time by leaving his scraps of paper. But, he could not say 'no' to Asha as she pestered him so much; he was married to her after all, and the bonds of marriage cannot be ignored.

Three months had slipped by since that event. They had gone to Gulmarg for over a week. A punjabi couple was already there in the hut that they had hired. Prakash too, spent a few days with them for he was a painter. He erected his easel under a pine tree and spent all his time in painting. Since women do not need much time to get acquainted with others, the two families were soon very intimate with each other. However, no one showed any interest in Prakash. The two families, except Asha, considered his passion for painting as just whiling away time. Asha was interested in old paintings, collected many, and got them pasted on the walls of her in-laws' house.

While he was spreading blue and yellow colours on the canvas, she appeared behind him.

'Are you too interested in painting?' Prakash asked her.

'Not much, I just love collecting paintings.' Asha replied smilingly.

'So we can say with confidence that there are people who value painters, and if nothing else, they house their works in their homes.' Prakash said while moving his brush on the canvas.

'People are just silly and stupid; you may forgive me for being rude, but this does not concern your family as they have some kind of interest in something at least. But my hosts do not show interest in anything but business. We expend our blood to represent some aspect of life on a little canvas. Yet there are stupid people who say that we waste our time.'

'May you please make a picture for me?'

'*Ha-ha-ha-ha* Surely. The pictures people ask me to do will be exhibited in a party at the house of one of my well-wishers on the coming Sunday. You too, stand invited by them on the occasion.'

'Really?'

'Do you know why they have invited you?' asked Prakash. 'Soon after the party, I shall make the picture that you want. However, you will have to promise me that you will not lose that picture anywhere. I am particular about that for I wish that people of future who might be interested in the works of art should be able to find some pictures here and there.'

On the next Sunday, there was a horde of people at Guptaji's house besides the members of the two families. The paintings were hung tidily on the walls. Most of the people left after tea without caring to look at the paintings. Professor L also left saying that he had just come home. Mr and Mrs Gupta, Asha, and Prakash were the only ones who stayed and saw the pictures one by one.

Mr Gupta sensed that Prakash seemed a little morose, he said, 'I think the time has yet to come when people are informed about art. You are rather ahead of your time.'

Prakash evinced a sarcastic smile and said, 'One must have a heart, two eyes and a brain to recognise the colours.'

'Now, will you please tell me what you aim at in this painting? It seems a harmony of certain colours.' Mr Gupta asked him.

Asha was quick to say, 'To me it is a slap on the insipidness of life.'

'Wow! Very good!' Prakash responded.

'People who have no sensation of smell cannot understand the combination of colours.'

'OK. Let's agree, but in this one rain, clouds, sunshine are all together. Where did they come from?' Mr Gupta asked him.

'A person who has not stayed in Gulmarg, and is not familiar with the changing weather of Gulmarg, cannot gain anything from this painting.' Prakash said. 'One who is not an admirer of nature is just like a buffalo hearing the melody of a bagpipe.'

Asha laughed, but controlled her laughter immediately as she thought that Mr Gupta might get irked.

She cast a glance at Guptaji's stupid wife, who was falling asleep.

Mr Gupta asked Asha, 'You might say that this image of the woman is clumsily drawn. Can it be called beautiful?'

'Yes certainly. I possess no mastery in painting, yet I can say that it hardly matters that the woman depicted is beautiful or not, it is evidently artistic.'

'How?' Mr Gupta asked her.

'It is because a woman possesses a passionate heart. Brother, one must have the eyes of the heart open to see an ocean of love surging from a woman's heart. But there is hardly anyone to give credit to the ocean. That might be the reason that she is rather poignant.' Prakash said.

'Mr Prakash.' The utterance came out from Asha's mouth.

Prakash got up and began gathering his paintings.

'People who do not dive deep into the heart of a woman,' he said, 'cannot find her hopes and aspirations.' Having gathered all the paintings, he lit a cigarette and went out. Asha followed him saying, 'Mr Prakash!'

'Asha, I empathise with you. How nice you are!'

'How do you… Who?...' Asha asked him while his head hung down.

'Do I simply idle my time here in Gulmarg? I fill my paintings with the hot blood of my heart instead of colours. An artist cannot appreciate how this is possible.'

'Give that picture to me, please.' Asha requested him.

'How can it be possible? It is the precious possession of my life - the apogee of my art.'

Being lost in such ruminations, Asha was surprised and got up; she discovered a new way of life, rather a spectacle, from this incident. She wiped her tears and mused that Prakash had been visiting their house since that event.

'Why did he continue coming here time and again? Does his coming here have any connection with my marriage?… No! Then! Why should I not approach him, touch his feet and say 'Prakash, please forgive me! I kept you waiting for me for so long.'

In the meantime, the servant came carrying a tray of tea. Having placed the cups on the three-legged stool, Asha said in rather a roaring way, 'Hello, take it away. Who am I here in this family? You go and keep your master entertained for the whole day.' Then she continued in an angry pitch, 'Go and serve this tea to the opium-addict of economics.'

'My lady, please give up your wrath. The bickering of

a husband and wife is short-lived like the showers of the rainy season that do not last long.'

Tears trickled down uncontrollably from Asha's eyes.

'Am I not having even this much of authority to sit near him and keep looking at him? Just looking at him? Your work is disturbed, *hunn*! Did I ruin my youth just to experience this moment? Go and tell him that I do not hanker after fame and money; I am rather thirsty for love and affection. I may satiate it wherever I want.'

She got up and tidied her hair, and the dhoti. She put on her slippers and then went near the servant.

'Please forgive me. I might have possibly been a little rude to you during the last few months.' She said to him and left. She paced hurriedly and reached Prakash's house. He was resting his elbow on the table and puffing his cigarette and spreading smoke. Seeing Asha there, he started. 'Oh! You! Namaste!' He said to her.

'Namaste!' Asha responded.

'It is your courage Ashaji,' said Prakash. 'How good you are!'

With tearful eyes Asha said, 'Please forgive me. I kept you waiting for so long.'

Amazed, Prakash got up and said to her, 'Waiting? Waiting for what?'

'Do not keep me yearning any further. I need your support. It is my luck that I have an admirer like you. I have relinquished Prof L's house.'

'You left your house? That is very bad of you. The world is like that.'

'Do not be sarcastic.' Asha was quick to tell him. 'I house only one desire in my heart that I might be able to love my husband to the best of my compassion. I shall surely do that after getting married to you.'

'Oh! Really? Me?' Prakash said rather gravely. 'Look madam, you have misunderstood me. Let me accompany you to your house.' Saying this Prakash went near the door and stood there.

'What do you mean?' Asha was flabbergasted and asked him.

'Look at me please. My being so candid with you in conversation does not mean that I am in love with you. Did you fancy that I was mad after you so I made a painting of you? You say that you might express your love only after marriage, don't you?'

'Yes.'

'Oh! In that case you refute what you say. You have falsely fallen in love with me. Where do your principles stand? Please forgive me. I do not want to cause you any humiliation.'

'So you do not love me?'

'Respected lady, love is not done, it just happens. May be you are in love, that is a different issue. As far as I am concerned, I have had this experience long back. It is the bitterness of that experience that has made me able to be what I am, that I can empathise with you.'

Asha felt stifled and stood transfixed like a wall of clay. A violent surge of tears welled up in her eyes. She was at a loss on what to do next. Since she had renounced her husband's house she could not survive there. She felt as if she had wantonly reached the middle of an unknown forest, and left many footprints after her. The bridle path that lay before her did not give her any inkling of her destination. She looked behind her but failed to identify even the bridle path that had led her to that blind end.

The Vein and the Pain

Dinanath, the watchman, was in a strange consternation. Someone had stirred the smouldering fire within him. He was wont to quibble with everyone. 'Someone has jinxed my morning', he thought, 'now the whole day shall prove very bad for me. God save me!'

He raised his right arm and looked at his right hand. He shook himself a couple of times, and then heaved a long sigh. He praised himself for this mad gesture, and his mind was filled with many bizarre ideas. Sometimes he laughed at what he had done early morning. He had cursed humanity, but soon felt penitent and said, 'Oh, I wish nobody had irked me!' He pondered over his actions and then felt as if his face, showing repentance and humility, appealed to humanity. Nevertheless, he did not want to mention the action to anyone. He considered silence to be proper, and retained it as a secret.

It was a morning of *Bhadrpad* (August), and cold breeze gave him freshness, yet he felt that the serenity of the air did not impart any freshness to his body. It felt like a flame that burnt every particle of his body with its heat. While placing his chin on the railing of the veranda of his office, he ruminated. His hookah lay on the ground; its fire-pot contained a part of the half-burnt tobacco and some of it was scattered on the cement floor. In the sunshine, the greenery of the compound brightened the quivering dew drops, much like his restive mind. The early morning event had agitated his mind. There were moments when he justified his action, but soon from some hidden recess of his mind arose a voice that shook him by saying, 'Your action was absolutely uncalled for.' Thus he grew more agitated.

'*Aa...chhih*! The meaningless words came to the tip of his tongue, and made his veins flutter. On hearing these words he felt as if some rabid dog had bit his leg. Of course the words were meaningless, but for him they implied a lot. The commuters who knew about his fear, smiled before saluting him, and soon after departing raised huge guffaws, repeating *Aa...chhih*! When Dinanath heard the words, his veins started fluttering, and a volley of curses came out from his mouth for them. 'God save me!... your sister's... *Atchoo*!! your mother's *Atchoo*! ... your daughter's *Atchoo*!*h*! And when he was busy in his work having no leisure to counter them, he called them names inwardly and took to his way. The accountant, the head clerk and others sitting in the office laughed uncontrollably, or raised intermittent guffaws which seemed to give relief to their hearts. But what affliction it caused to Dinanath was known to none but him.

A similar episode had taken place today. He came across a Muslim young man in the office premises. When they departed after exchanging greetings, the young man called him some slang name. On hearing it, Dinanath felt as if his body was being crushed in the grinding mill, like the one yonder the bridge ahead. He ran after him, seized him and slapped him with full strength that made the young man's nose bleed. Seeing this he stood transfixed in shock. This action continued to vex him. In order to ward off this vexation, he raised his right arm and shook it violently as if he wanted to get rid of something nasty stuck to it.

He worked as a watchman in the public works office. A tall young man with a thin physique and sunken cheeks. He was neither beautiful nor ugly. His nose was long and eyes sunk in their sockets. Although he was fragile in terms of his body frame, but he possessed enough strength in his muscles. The turban made of green cotton cloth was never off his head; the black streaks of dirt were visible to all. Although he was tall, he walked with short and quick steps and as such, was noticed by all those who walked on the road. When someone irked him, a weird situation was caused.

His head always remained bent towards his right shoulder. He always greeted everyone he met with a humble gesture of holding his two hands together. And if the person was a Muslim, he greeted by saying *Assalamualaikum*. If per chance he felt that the situation was in his favour, he was happy, and his face brightened by his inner joy as if he had found that which he had ever hankered after.

Dinanath always talked to everyone with a smiling face, be it the accountant, the head clerk, the treasurer or any other office bearer. He was courteous to everyone and addressed them as '*Mahara*' (Sir), even if they were children or their domestic helps. Many times he did not even say 'no' if he was asked to do cooking at their homes. Whenever it was an auspicious day, he was engaged in house-work; he was confident this demeanour could help him get some clout with his officers, or some other favour. He was sure that sooner or later, he would be elevated from a watchman to an orderly. At the same time, he knew it well that all his seniors in the office knew his weaknesses, yet he felt ecstatic when they said a word to him in a grave mood. Yet the employees of the treasury enjoyed provoking him and cause some kind of a boisterous event; they laughed loudly at him and their laughter pierced his heart. This was the reason he made sure that he reached the office at 9 o'clock in the morning and fancied newer incidents. He always felt that his life was about to revolve around a new pivot, and thus he laughed to himself, but soon got lost in gloomy thoughts.

Generally, he never quibbled with anyone nevertheless, all his strength of tolerance had petered out. Many a time he was advised to feign deafness to all the provocations. He tried his best to follow the advice, but realised soon that his nonchalance to provocations was an insult to his manliness. He would lose patience and utter rude slangs.

He recollected the event in his life that had led him to the present mental agony. One day while he visited the market in the town, his very presence caused gossip among the onlookers. A Sardar who dealt in ghee stood up when Dinanath passed his shop. While moving his hand on his protruding belly he said, '*Sat sri akal maharaj*!' Dinanath walked ahead calmly. As soon as he walked away, the Sardar took out an empty ghee can and started beating it. In the next shop, a businessman rapt in his accounts, started on hearing the clamour. He left his accounts book and started uttering '*Atchoo*! *Atchoo*!' In no time a din of '*Atchoo*! *Atchoo*!' could be heard from all the shops. This made Dinanath think that all of them were plunderers who would bare him of all his clothing and make him stand nude amidst the market. Making a miserable face he looked at each one of them. When no one relented, he burst into a volley of curses.... The remembrance of all such events kept him ruminating. He assessed every event in minute detail in all possible ways. Soon, he remembered that the oafs and ruffians sitting in the porches of the village shops always found some kind of excuse to provoke his rancour. While thinking about them he finally concluded that all of them were bastards.

Absorbed in such musings, he raised his head a little and gave up the support of his right hand. Now his eyes were absorbed in the deep sky yonder the copses. The sound of the slow-moving waters of the *Madhumati* stream intensified his anguish.

He thought that if his father were living, his lot would

have been different. No one would have dared to taunt him for he belonged to a Pundit family. All the Pundits in the town depended on the power of his father. But today, the son of the same Pundit was jeered by street urchins, vagabonds, and worth nothing workers of shopkeepers. He laughed loudly: *Ha-ha-ha-*! But the laughter was an amalgam of whines and placidity. He was no lunatic who could be mocked. His eyes caught sight of the awkwardly trimmed log-like mulberry tree standing on the opposite bank of the Madhumati River; soon after evening, many owls hooted from that tree.

He felt as if it was already evening and from a bare bole of the mulberry tree some owl screamed, took wings to go to his house to scream there. His face and nose contorted with anger as if the call of the owl caused unbearable pain in every part of his body. For a moment he remembered the event of his mother's death. In spite of all this he could see no light in the bright Sun. May be it was an assertion of good tidings that the future would be guided by reason. But what befell him that he was so miserable? Why did he behave as a timid and superstitious person? Why did the people of the town harass him? For a moment he held himself responsible for all his misery. 'It might be that I myself am cynical about the new times. It might be that it is the result of my sins that I suffer endlessly.' All these musings caused a strange consternation in his mind. He realised that he stood at a crossroad of his life, stricken by forebodings! He laughed again that caused an echo near the veranda: *ha-ha-ha- hi - hi- hi-*

It was a routine with the employees of the office that they organised a party whenever an employee was included in the fraternity of the head clerk, treasurer, accountant or any other employee of the Public Works Department. Only a couple of days ago, a munshi of the Revenue Office had joined them, and he too was to be included in the fraternity with a party, and the party was to be given in his honour in the evening.

Dinanath, the watchman, thought that when he was engaged in cooking, the officials joining the party had started giggling. Their children sitting near them tried to get an acclaim by uttering '*Atchoo*! *Atchoo*!...!' and looked towards their parents. But the new munshi joining the office knew nothing about the secret. He looked at everyone with amazement. A gossip monger informed the new member about the secret. But on being informed, he grew sympathetic towards Dinanath. But how could he know that emotions of pity and mercy had already overwhelmed the mind of the new employee who was transferred to the office? Nobody in the fraternity informed him that the emotion would soon vanish from his mind. Oh, could the accountant make him understand that all this was being done for the one who considered logical reasoning as ludicrous. Thus, the new entrant came to understand that there was certainly some secret that agonised Dinanath's heart.

'Look here, kids, this does not become you.' The accountant, who earlier whirled like a spin top, was heard admonishing the kids, yet his mute smile evinced that he was in fact encouraging them. The uttering of '*Atchoo*! *Atchoo*!...!' made the new employee envision the young and old folks of Srinagar town and its markets. He thought how innocent lives were being crushed in the markets. Dinanath, however, was lucky to be away from Srinagar, much distanced from the urban culture. 'I should grow intimacy with Dinanath and express my sympathy to him.' Soon after the new munshi left, he calmly walked towards his residence. Hoping to gain his sympathy, he called him to the door of his flat:

'Mahaldaar Sahab!'

Hearing the call, the munshi stood up and looked out to find that he was the person who was engaged in cooking and was now free. He thought that he came to get acquainted with him. The munshi said, 'Tell me, my brother, what is the matter.'

He sat down calmly and in the light of the burning lantern, he looked like a pitiable tramp. Perhaps his purpose of visiting the munshi was achieved. He was almost nonplussed to see a queer glow and glory on the munshi's face; he thought he was pitying him but the munshi wanted to say to Dinanatha, 'Lucky watchman, think about your personal life. Your life is very precious, and a source of comfort for all the others around you. If you were not there in the office, even the willows would stop their whispering. Who is there to do all the chores of cooking for the new officials?'

He said aloud, 'Watchman, Dinanath!'

Dinanath had left. Today in the morning, while thinking

about his lot, he recollected that he had left the munshi's house without telling him anything or hearing a word from him. Keeping the purpose of visiting him concealed in his mind, he got up and again went to the munshi's residence.

Dinanath stood at the crossroads, at a new turn in his life. He had a feeling of real interest in life that arose and abated in his mind, but re-appeared after subsiding. Nevertheless, his eyes evinced a little red hue and moisture. His eyes suggested as if the gushing waters of the canyon swept away the bridge, but his companions had already reached the opposite bank. He was the only one having a sense of defeat for having missed the chance of crossing the canyon over the bridge.

'Babuji, please scribe an application that the personnel in the office are not good human beings and they never feel any compunction in annoying me.'

The munshi remained silent. He wished to beseech him, 'Munshi Sahab, write in the application that I resign from service for I want to go to such a place where no one harasses me.' On the contrary, the munshi wanted to tell him that human nature is all the same everywhere. If you decide to leave this village, your tormentors will not let you leave. They shall surround you wherever you are.My mother and my wife have decided that we shall leave this village and settle at a place where there are no loafers and brutish shopkeepers. 'Please write it Babuji. My heart is restless.'

The munshi took a leaf of paper and pen in his hand and started writing. Watchman Dinanath noticed him writing and thought to submit his resignation and flee the place. But instead of a resignation application, the munshi wrote his transfer letter in which he wrote precisely but strong words about his condition, and recommended that Dinanath be transferred to some other location.

He approached the engineer and submitted his letter.

In the evening he visited the munshi's residential quarters to express his gratitude. 'Munshi Sahab, I can never forget the favour that you have done to me. The engineer promised to transfer me very soon.' Having said these words, he giggled again: *hi..hi..hi..* 'Munshi Sahab… your kindness… *hi..hi..hi..* How gracious you are… the personnel of my own office…'

Having heard laughter, some vagabonds of the locality came in and started raising a din. Dinanath went away while spewing foul abuses.

When the cows were returning home after having grazed to their full, the noise of the goats and sheep could be heard, rising and then falling. The crows flew to their nests and the smoke rising from the village was absorbed in the space. All of a sudden, the whole ambience was polluted, and a din was heard. Dinanath was running while carrying two big stones in his hands. Two men chased him. 'Catch hold of him… stop him… hold him…!' The person who had met him in the morning appeared and caught hold of him. In the meantime, a huge bevy of people surrounded him.

The turban on Dinanath's head disappeared. His trousers were torn up to his thighs. The front of his shirt was torn, leaving his belly denuded, and his naked body bore many injury marks at various places. Blood drops trickled from his mouth. He uttered weird sounds: *'Aa chhinh Aaa chhinh...!'* that he kept repeating. He squatted in the middle of the road, and while laughing boisterously, he beat his face by his two hands. People felt scared to go near him. Some voices could distinctly be heard amidst the noise:

'He has axed his own feet. Had not the poor fellow sneezed at the time of leaving, the calamities would not have befallen him. Superstitious! Funk!'

The new munshi walked speedily towards the reception. He thought, 'I wish the engineer had issued the transfer order of the watchman.' He realised that it was not fortunate but now it was the right time to discuss the issue.

Dinanath was actually transported to an altogether different world - a world where he was supposed to keep raising loud guffaws; remain immune to taunts, and never bother about others' teasing him. He was absolutely free now.

At the Crossroads

Taravati, having worked throughout the day was wearied and sat propped up against the wall, heaving long sighs; every part of her body ached. In order to relax, she stretched her legs and pressed them with her hands. Seeing her feet covered with dust, she sighed again. She mused, 'My big plump feet are cracked. Like them, my life too, has started getting emaciated.'

She got up, and gave a call through the window, 'Roopa! O Roopa!' Having called Roopa a couple of times, she sat again on the ground. All the things that she had collected were scattered in the room. Her daughter Roopa was to take her examination from the next day. Taravati had borrowed a stove from one of her neighbours and utensils from some other neighbour: a bucket from one and a tripod from some other. Thus, she managed to collect all the essential things for Roopa's cooking test.

All of a sudden Taravati remembered her husband. The dispersed things on the floor reminded her of every word that her deceased husband had said. 'Roopa's mother, why do you seem to be possessed? Why are you adamant to take away life from her little body? Let me fetch you a pouch of poison ... Are there only sons that deserve to be called your children? I shall make sure that she gets the best of education. I wish you too were an educated woman! You would have not thought about this goofy thing then. Look at me. Never thrash her.' While rapt in such recollection, her eyes were filled with tears. Her husband nagged her at every excuse. Many times the couple sulked and even stopped talking to each other after a trivial issue. It often happened that when she banged Roopa, her husband immediately rebuked her. On such occasions, she wore her head cloth, tied a *lungi* over her *pheran*, the Kashmiri outer garment, and rushed to her paternal house and stayed there for several weeks. Thus, Roopa was the cause of all bickering between them. But, all the same, it was Roopa only who made them come together as well. At the time of breathing his last, Taravati's husband wept bitterly for he feared that after his death she might hit his daughter more severely. He held Roopa close to his chest and said to Taravati, 'Please fulfil every demand that Roopa makes after my death.'

Taravati wiped her tears from her face.

The elongated shadows had covered all the surroundings outside. Taravati felt a mild headache. She again noticed her dust-covered feet, and engaged herself in tidying the utensils and the other things strewn about. She wanted to finish tidying the room and then wash her feet in hot water that would alleviate her fatigue of the day. In one quick movement, she stood up and called through the widow:

'Roopa! Listen, O Roopa!'

A voice came from the nearby house, 'I am coming in a moment, Mom.'

'Now please be home as early as possible. See how long I have been waiting for you!' Then she called her again. After that she talked to herself, 'Whenever I search for her, she is at Sheela's house. Is she bothered about her own self or others? How many times have I admonished her not to go there, but she always turns deaf ears to me. What trash will she learn from that clumsy woman? Here I am tired after a whole day, and she! She hardly bothers. I could have heated the water in the meantime, but I keep waiting for this daughter of mine to come. What can I expect from her? Sooner or later, she will go to her husband's house....'

In spite of all this, she loved her daughter Roopa for she had anchored her hopes in her. Roopa was the only human being she could call her own. She alone cared for her. Her husband's last heart-wrenching words had brought Roopa closer to Taravati.

While her husband lived, she opposed Roopa's going to school; it was a bizarre thing in her life that her daughter would go to school. Wearing high healed sandals, doing her hair daily, and crossing limits in sprucing herself; she had never seen such things in her youth. She remembered that era very well when her mother took pains to teach her to pound paddy in the mortar. And when she got married, she would cleanse more than a *maund* of rice from morning to evening. She dung-plastered her house at least twice in a week, yet she never failed to do all her other chores. She did not have leisure to read books or, like school boys do left-right and play and romp. She still remembered that she had never talked in friendly terms with her mother-in-law until her death; there was no question of laughing, frolicking, and guffawing in her presence.

She mused that it was only in the last ten to fifteen years that girls had started going to school; once there were schools exclusively for boys, now a topsy-turvy had happened. Some girls became doctors, some teachers and many became nurses. Eh! A sacred place like Kashmir too has become a place of vulgarity.

She loved Roopa passionately, and sacrificed all comforts and joy for her. Nevertheless, she would not let her have too much freedom that would cause her ruin. She was convinced that girls of her time are easily led astray, but as soon as she espied Sheela, she was in a fix for she was not misguided till then. She roamed about freely and there was certainly some kind of broadness of mind in her that Roopa was yet to acquire.

In the meantime, Roopa entered. She was a tall and thin girl, much like a maze plant, and possessed a slender waste with a wheatish hue. She rejoiced when she saw the items she needed. She said with a joyous dangle, 'Mataji, you have got all the things that I needed. You are really nice.' Then she checked all the items one by one. Seeing the gloomy face of her mother, she went near her and started massaging her legs. Taravati, with her eyes half-closed, lay backwards. A slight smile danced on her lips.

Roopa said, 'Mataji, Sheela asked me which school I would join after passing my examination. She also told me that there is a very good way of teaching in Arya School.'

'Let her utter this nonsense. The girls of the present times hardly bother. Now take all these items and keep them tidily. We will think over this issue only after the examinations are over. Look here, you know, you are a grown up girl now.' Her mother said to her calmly.

'No mother, I shall take care of these items later, let me first heat water to wash your feet. And I shall also prepare *Qahva* for you.' Saying this she got up. Taravati cast a searching look at her from her head to feet. She was now in her early youth - a fourteen year old girl. She stood like a statue in front of her. The mother had noticed a little bulging on her chest yesterday, but today it was not there. She was amazed.

'Look at me. Come closer to me, here, and sit to my right.' She said to Roopa and while remaining stretched on the floor, she pulled a corner of her trousers to make her sit. Roopa was quick to know that her mother's eyes were fixed on her chest. She understood this and lowered her eyes in modesty. Taravati, too, realised and holding her by her arm, said with an intent look,

'Oh… this…?'

'Yes, mother, I am wearing a bra. It helps to...' Roopa could not say anything more for being coy. How could she tell her mother that wearing a bra gave her joy, gave her satisfaction; besides it helped in concealing the bulging of breasts to some extent?

Seeing her bashful looks and a sudden reddish flash on her face, Taravati grew restive. She wished to know what the queer thing a bra was like; she had spent her whole life in her loose *Pheran*. She was wonderstruck on hearing the very word brassieres, but at the same time she grew happy. In her youth she desperately tried to hide her bulging breasts from the ogling eyes of strangers each time she was drenched in perspiration because of her bashfulness. The vibrations of her breasts always invited the attention of all onlookers. She thought, 'Roopa, too, could make an exhibition of her breasts without wearing any brassieres. Then what made her wear it?' Then she recollected an episode that Roopa had told her one day on her return from school, 'Mother, when a boy blocked the way of my friend Chanda, I took my slippers and thrashed him. I hit him so much that he fled like a smoke-driven mouse.'

At that moment Taravati had wondered how her Roopa had possessed so much strength and showed such courage. In her youth, she had never had even a word with any young man. She invoked evil upon Roopa's going to school and cursed her. But today she was happy that Roopa possessed the virtue of modesty.

A thought occurred to her. Since the time their

neighbour's daughter started going to college, she had developed a strange simplicity. Before her joining the college she had never missed anything in her make-up and donning, but she was a little girl then. Now, she did not show that girlish joy in her show off; her life had started afresh and she did not go perverse. But every girl could not be like Sheela. She inferred that only books could have such an influence on their character.

Soon many other weird ideas occurred to her. She envisioned Roopa as a youthful girl: an idol of her father's ambitions. She was now a complete woman, but much different from Taravati? In terms of her wisdom and discerning, she was like a statuette made of hard core metal that could not be broken or reshaped by anyone. She imagined her as a fragile flower that could not be trampled by anyone. She had never deviated from the path of virtue. But the reality of the statuette had refuted the old idea and fear that canopied Taravati's mind and that of numerous women like her. 'Am I an obstacle in the path of Roopa? Am I forcing her to go perverse? No...no. I will not allow Roopa to pursue her education after her examination.'

While she was lost in various premonitions and ruminations, Roopa entered with hot water to wash her feet. After savouring a cup of *Qahva*, Taravati reclined to a corner of the room. Roopa tied the scarf on her mother's head, tidied all the things around her, and placed a book in front and sat near her mother's pillow to read.

The next day the examinations started; she was

already well disposed to appear in it. She had got her new *Saree* dyed pink, got it glued, and had polished her sandals at Sheela's house. She had washed her shirt and trousers early in the morning. But Taravati was gripped by another anxiety.

'Roopa, how far away is the venue of the examination?' Taravati asked.

'It is just a little distance away from the first bridge. Sheela told me that Krishna will accompany me as he goes to his college in the same direction.' Roopa replied.

Taravati started at the name of Krishna. She said again. 'Roopa, I have told you a thousand times that it is not good to talk to boys of other houses. How many more times should I warn you?'

'Krishna is Sheela's brother, and as such, mine too. All the girls of the locality call him brother. You talk weird things!'

Yet Taravati did not appreciate this. She was about to resolve that she would accompany Roopa to the centre. She envisioned all the faces of the girls of the neighbourhood. Many of them were forced by their parents to keep indoors. Kamala's mother, in a casual conversation, had once said to her, 'Kamala is now able to read and write to some extent. She is even able to read and write letters in Hindi. What else does she want?' She had thus in a way convinced Taravati to stop Roopa's education there and then.

In their locality, majority of the girls were like Kamala, they could read and write letters and other chits. Most of the letters hardly meant anything. The category of such girls was quite distinct. And Sheela's world was altogether different, and that of Roopa's too. She too, avoided being included in that category that she execrated.

The next day, when Roopa accompanied by Krishna, returned from the examination centre, Taravati did not ask her anything about the examination, but was quick to say, 'Why are you so late?' Then she stared at Roopa's face as if probing for something secret. Roopa, on the other hand, wanted her mother to ask about her performance in the examination wherein she would give her a cheerful reply.

Taravati thought it was no trivial thing to be late in coming home. Roopa, too, had made a perfect assessment of the time while leaving her house: half an hour from her home to the examination centre and half an hour for the return: she had left at seven o'clock in the morning and was back by quarter past eleven. Taravati was gripped by strange hunches when she was late by fifteen minutes: 'Who knows that she....' On the contrary, Roopa was sure that she was home on time. She did not mind her mother remaining rashly silent because she was convinced that she was not late. She finally told her mother, 'Mataji, you did not ask me anything about my examination! I performed well.'

Not disposed to reply, yet a couple of words came out from Taravati's mouth, 'That might be the reason that it took you longer time.'

Roopa remained calm for she had to take the cooking test the next day.

On the second day of Roopa's examination, Taravati

herself accompanied her to the centre. She had to keep waiting there for a pretty long time until Roopa came out from the hall. She carried most of the kitchen items herself, and gave only a little of it to her mother to carry. But instead of asking her daughter anything about her performance, she was busy in watching the people in the street who looked at them. Observing their grimaces, she felt her legs growing frail. She started reflecting, 'All these folks are sure to be mothers and fathers of one or the other daughters.' She did not consider it courteousness that some of the men ogled at Roopa. 'Loafers! Lascivious men, who seduce young and innocent girls and then kidnap them.'

She knew about many incidents of seduction of innocent girls; she tried to recollect all those incidents. A girl-friend of Roopa's came across to meet her, and she eventually walked faster leaving her mother behind.

When she reached Hari Singh High Street, she called Roopa to stop there. Roopa might not have heard her call, and so she did not look behind. This irked Taravati who concluded that education had made Roopa arrogant.

'Why does Roopa not walk by her mother's side? How does it matter that my dupatta is worn out and that my heels are cracked? And...' She soon recollected what Kamala's mother had said to her. She hated Sheela's naivety. At that moment she forgot that Sheela too had possessed the same kind of conceitedness at this stage of her life, and the same conceit had now changed into simplicity. Inwardly, she resolved that she would stop

Roopa's education. It was enough that she is able to read and write. She could at least use it in writing letters to her maternal uncle. Taravati was sure that she had agreed to what her late husband had requested her.

'At least I complied with what he asked me to do and I let Roopa have some education. Although she could not be a complete woman, it is by no means an ordinary thing that she is able to write something or the other in a clumsy, but readable way.'

The examination was over. Taravati raised the issue with Roopa. It was no less than crumbling of a mountain over Roopa. She thought of many other girls of her neighbourhood – Kamala, Janaki, Prabha and others. She knew it well that they were called various types of names in the locality. They looked like those winged birds who desperately strike the bars of their cages with their beaks to be free. 'Their vision knows nothing of the open. They are like the frogs in a well.' She assessed their condition one by one and wished to be away from the lot. 'If I too become like one of them...'

When Taravati stubbornly refused to let her continue her education, Roopa wept bitterly. Somehow she mustered courage when she thought about her new girl-friends. She reflected that though their brains had not matured, they were illiterate, but at least they could read and write letters.

Taravati was more alert in keeping a watch on Roopa's activities. Nevertheless, Roopa chanced to meet her friends while fetching water from the public water point in the street; she liked conversing with them, revealing her woes and hearing theirs. She also did not give up visiting Sheela's house. She was absolutely idle; her immature and delicate brain too was idle. Her mother's constant vigil was sure to leave some impression on her. She had no anxiety about her studies as her mother's decision was unchanging. Her girl-friends thronged around her; they too had hardly found any chance to breathe in the open atmosphere and inhale fresh air. She sensed some kind of smell in their company, but she had no option but to breathe it in. She felt like she was being pressed down in the water, but she was like a bole that re-emerged and stretched out whenever she was forced to sink.

Taravati noticed that Roopa had abandoned wearing the bras. She asked her, 'Why did you put out your bras?' Roopa was already annoyed, and thus said harshly, 'Why should I wear it while sitting indoors? Alright, I might wear it when the need arises.' By the word 'need' she meant satiation of sexual desires and feelings of pleasure and attraction.

Taravati remembered Sheela again who had never deviated from the right path. On the day when Roopa was to appear in the examination, she had sneered at Sheela's naïveté; she was feeling bad about it, but Roopa's aplomb and verve had defeated her. She wished that her daughter wore her bras in keeping with the norms of modesty. Roopa, on the other hand, wanted to know from her that how did she expect it from her daughter when she herself had not even heard the name of the thing.

In the evening, when Roopa was going to the public

water point to fetch water, her mother called her; she did not let her have time to even share a word with her friends. And when she was home, Taravati was rather harsh to her, 'Roopa, your symptoms are not good. It is evening time, and you know that thieves are at large in the evening. Don't you have this much sense? What will happen if any one does some mischief?'

Roopa was already simmering with anger, and the flames were inclined to engulf her.

During her schooling years, she had no inkling of her destination, but now she found it very close to her - a new path gave her the idea of her destination. She stealthily stared at youthful boys and had weird ideas about them. The boys too loved her in the world of their dreams and fancies. She always kept herself trimmed and spruced. She felt herself akin to that veiled princess who made wayfarers heave sighs and wished that she would remove the veil at least once. She was convinced that even after getting an education, her destination might not be different than where she found herself. A woman is ultimately a woman; her feminine sexual desires cannot vanish.

One day Taravati called Roopa from the nearby market, 'Roopa here is a letter from your maternal uncle. The postman gave it to me in the street. Take it and read it out to me.'

Roopa opened the letter, and looking at it, she grew restive.

'Is he well?' Taravati asked her.

'Yes mother, he is quite well, but he is anxious about my examination... I shall write a reply to him.'

Saying this she got up. Her face had reddened. She entered the room in front of her, closed the door from inside and said to herself,

'My maternal uncle's letter!...*hahhaha*... I cheated my mother. I called Shama's letter *Maama's* letter!'

There was turmoil in her mind. She opened it again and read it. And then she moved her head in negation. She wanted to tear the letter, but in the meantime, a smile danced on her face. The same smile appeared in the form of ecstasy. Finally, she crumbled the letter in her fist and held it close to her chest. 'Oh my dear Shama!' She was so happy as if she had embraced Shama, not his letter. Her heart accepted Shama's call, and she started writing a reply to Shama.

The Custody

'Get me a mouth organ... Get me *pakoras*... (Fried fritters) Why don't you?'

The child was stubborn while standing behind Ramnath and shaking his shoulders. Ramnath shook like a child lulled in its mother's lap and the child is solaced, delighted and smiling. However, Ramnath did not smile as he was annoyed by the child's stubbornness. A bundle of official documents lay in front of him that he had got home for he could not complete the work in his office. He was keen to complete his work, but the naughty child's *uun..uun* changed his decision.

'Won't you get me? Why not? I will take away your spectacles.' He was about to remove his father's spectacles. Ramnath got up and shoved him, and the child fell down on the floor. But he was quick to stand up, and came near his father; he was yet to give up his demands. His father slapped him, so harshly that the child's nose bled. He cried aloud. Ramnath's youthful eyes reddened like lamps. He had hardly entered his house that the child appeared in front of him. He pestered him like a tame dog of a stranger's house always follows you, annoys you. He thought that Radha too has a child, and Sobhavati has not one but three—'How many children can I count, there are numerous children in the locality, but God save all from a child like this! No sooner is he out of bed in the morning, than his demand for money starts, and when I leave my house he is again after money. If not money, he demands a mouth organ, or *pakora*. I am afraid he might keep chewing *pakoras* for his whole life as if life is nothing without a mouth organ or *pakoras* - I wonder how long I will keep meeting the demands of my family. Kishna needs mouth organ and *pakora*s, and Shama keeps weeping for not getting a new frock. The elbows of Shankar's coat are worn out. And there is Krishna's itching in her head and Jamna needs her English primer – She must get pickles and fruit every day. Ever since she conceived again, she has made me a pauper. And it is still the advent of her youth, God knows...' He kept musing. '*Eenn..eenn...uun...uun... mommy! uunn... uunn...*'

The child was still crying while his nose bled; even his hands were drenched with blood. Ramnath looked back and seeing the child's condition felt ashamed of himself. Oh blood! He felt that the child played holy for harmonium and *pakoras.* He stood in front of his son and tried to calm his nerves. His lips were dry, and his feet shrunk.

'I was just trying to silence the child,' he said smilingly but his tongue and the accent!

In the meantime his lucky wife entered bearing a *Samovar* of boiling tea. Seeing the crying child she started beating her chest.

'Who has beaten you? I will sacrifice my life for you. Oh Ram! Blood!' She was about to drop the boiling Samovar from her hands, when Ramnath held it. Her eyes were blood red with anger and entire body shaking. She saw her son crying while drenched in blood. The blood stains on his face looked frightening; some had already dried. Having observed this, the child's father was nonplussed.

'Are you happy now? Catch hold of him and slay him. You consider him a mute sheep rather than your son! Do you read this very stuff in your hefty books? Oh Rama!' Then she cried while raising a huge noise.

Ramnath maintained his reticence, perhaps ashamed of his behaviour. But how could he relieve himself of this guilt by saying that the child pestered him by demanding money and *pakora*s. How could the things be called important? 'I wish I had got him the things, the issue would not have become so complicated then.' He wished to get up and touch his wife's feet and with folded hands tell her, 'Oh my goddess, forgive me. Just have a look at my total income and expenditures. You would easily come to know that I have never splurged money. Oh yes, Jeevan Lal and Madhusudan took, rather dragged me, to the cinema, and when it was my turn to pay for the tickets, how adroitly I had avoided them. Today I am sick, tomorrow I might have to arrange for the wood fuel. Then I have so much work to attend to in my office. No, no, today I must take them to the cinema. I do not want to remain burdened by their generosity; after all I too have to take care of my honour. Let Kishna weep a thousand times. It is just his childishness, and all children keep weeping even if they are provided with love and care. Weeping is a part of children's nature, be they quarrelsome or gentle. Weeping is their origin as they come to this world while crying. What makes them different is that one is satiated by plenty of milk in his/her mother's breasts, and others suck the shrivelled breast of their mother to make them ooze out blood drops instead of milk. And thus remain weeping for his/her entire life.'

He was not inclined to think whether his children too enjoyed any pampering in his house.

Subhagyavati said to him while weeping, 'Did I yearn for anything for myself? Just go to Radha's house and see for yourself how much her husband cares about her and the children. I choke the innocent children whenever they demand anything. But I am afraid you will never go to see for yourself. Her husband drops a whole rupee in the hands of every child that approaches him when he is going to office. And then when he is home in the evening, he fetches something or the other for each of them. But see what happens here: even an affectionate word is not shared with our children. If you are really annoyed by their demanding nature, catch hold of each of them and finish your problem by slitting their throats. Yes, get up, get up …'

Ramnath could no longer contain himself and said in reply: 'You are irked for nothing. I slapped him a bit wrongly, and you make a hill out of a mole's grain.'

His wife said in a more agitated mood while wiping tears from her face, 'Yes, yes, you slapped him at a wrong place. You could even kick his eyes so that he would remain confined at one place forever. You should have banged him on his teeth, so that he could never chew *pakora*s and be contented with rice water. Or you should have punched both his ears so that … '

'Do not poke your nose in my affairs. The child belongs to me as well. He has become crazy. And who else should mend him? Do not approach me with your wisdom.'

Ramnath said all this to her, only to be free from his hidden fright. 'If today we encourage his trivial demands, tomorrow he might indulge in robbery. The folks will call him by a hundred names, and you will finally approach the police while beating your chest.'

His wife left the room, taking her weeping son along with her. The child was still crying and she tried to calm him, 'My Kishna, you should not become a habitual weeping child. Look there! A policeman! .... A thief... Ok. Let me tell you a fairy tale.' She was scared of her husband's talk. She used the word 'policeman' only to suppress the child's emotions, but the child was too obdurate to listen to her.

'Is it true that a child's unfulfilled demands lead him to become a burglar in his youth? Is it true that all children who yearn for trivial things and are not satiated in their childhood turn out to be dacoits when they grow up? And those who nurse their ambitions, do they really fulfil them?' In fact her husband had made her conscious of a fact of life.

He was convinced that such children definitely turn out to be dacoits. 'But who is the target of their burglary? Perhaps those who suppress their aspirations, and trample their emotions, are the targets. But with what face do they appear as dacoits?' While lost in such musings, Ramnath envisioned their faces: 'May be load-carrying labourers, Ramnath and his clerks, those operating machine drivers, or menials who tug vehicles - all of them are grouped in one category. They include people whose ambitions are already dead, who have no ambition in their lives, and do not aim at any destination, who are humbled for being helpless and powerless. They keep their hopes, ambitions and aspirations interred deep inside their bosoms. They are always grateful to others and never express any grudge.'

Sinking and rising in forebodings like these, he appeared to have a dream: he dreamt that Kishna had become a young man, and at the same time he dreamt that Radha's child too had grown up: one without any aspiration and the other having infinite. 'Kishnanlal, if you do not agree to work, we might find many others in your place.

'Sir, if I do not work, what shall I eat?' After all, I also have self-respect! Today I am really ashamed!

'No, no. What then? Your father was our neighbour, but these whims and shams will not work anymore.'

'No, Sir, please have trust in me, I will never be so negligent in future.'

While having such frightful musings, Ramnath felt as if his head was hammered, and the spell of the dream shattered.

'*Hahahaha*! Should I repress the ambitions of my children? What shall be the result? Oh! What to do now? Shall Radha's son make my Kishna a slave to fulfil his ambitions? No. It is simply impossible. I shall strengthen my son Kishna's ambitions. I shall tell him, "My dear child, I shall fetch you whatever you ask for. Do not worry. My dear gem, do not weep. I shall get a new coat for Shankar. Let me ready myself in arranging all the clothing for your younger brother who is yet to be born. I shall arrange a nurse for him. You are in no way a lesser child than Shobhavati's children. Now tell me what items do you need? Tell me, I shall make a list of them. Okay, *pakoras*, toys, copper coins, mouth organ, a bicycle, a motor and... Keep telling me." What about Shama and Krishna? Their husbands too might be the masters of their decisions. They too might be good guys like you. But, please do not be dacoits? No, no. I am wrong...Oh, no one shall become a dacoit or a burglar, if all the needs, ambitions and aspirations are fulfilled within the limits of proportion. A deep river always has a placid surface; it neither swells up nor does it produce tides.'

Having reflected so much, he began to make resolutions, 'For the present, I shall get the English primer for Shama and medicine for Krishna's itch-cure, and for your mother, I shall get a daily cake of butter, bread, fruit and calcium. In addition to that, *Chutni* and pickle that make pregnant women's mouths water. How much does it amount to?... OK. For you, I shall get *pakoras* and copper coin. But Jivan Lal and Madhusudan had come just now. I will not ask them for any favour, I shall not degrade my position in their eyes. How does it matter that they forced me twice to accompany them to the cinema? But I am not the one to demean myself for a few coins. Sooner or later, I shall invite them to some show in a cinema hall. Tomorrow is the first day of the new month. All shall end up smoothly.'

He came out of the room. He felt a new kind of vision in his eyes, a new light, and his face shone with real joy. After taking some steps, he turned towards his room. He again moved away, but returned. He finally took out a rupee from the inner pocket of his coat; it was a new coin that felt hot in his warm palm. He had a strange feeling of having passionate love for his child that made him restive and impatient to go jump near him.

He moved towards the room on the ground floor where all his kindred stayed. Their faces did not evince any sign of anxiety or woe. In fact, he wanted to express his humility to his wife and praise her parsimonious way of spending. He stepped down the stairs with loud thuds. Having reached the last step, he stopped near the door and tried to eavesdrop. He heard his child's weeping change into whines, while the face of the child's mother appeared bright with joy. He calmly listened in. The lugubrious tone of Krishna's mother too had changed. She laughed merrily while talking to somebody. 'Oh, yes, it is Radha.' He recognised her voice. 'Has she come to know about all that happened in the house? Perhaps not. She might have come now. How does it matter? Let her know that after all Ramnath too is doing something for his children. Let me first of all drop the new coin in the child's hand. Subhagyavati is never tired of talking high of Radha's affluence. Let Radha know today that people of our status also know how to show affection among the family members as much as Radha's husband has for her. Perhaps, she might not understand that although Ramnath loves Krishna, but that has reached repletion in Radha's presence. Radha's love is eternal as it gets revealed in fulfilling the needs of her children.'

Before entering, Ramnath gave out a call, 'Kishna, O Kishna.' It caused silence inside the room; there was no response to his call.

'Kishna!... O Kishna's mom?'

Still there was no reply. Thus he entered the room.

'Kishna dear, come with me.' He hugged the dear child and placed the rupee-coin in his hand… 'You keep this rupee ...'

Diverting Radha's attention, he said to her, 'You know my dear sister, kids, after all....*hahahaah*.... I shall take him to the bazaar. Come, let us go to the bazaar where I shall get you many good things.'

With a sarcastic smile on her face, Radha looked towards Subhagyavati, the latter blushed for some reason. She said ironically to Ramnath, 'So you ingratiate a sulking child by giving him Rupee One! Here is the child's mother too sulking, get something or the other to please her as well. Okay, if it is not one whole Rupee, let it be half of it. *Hahaha*.. Let it be a bottle of oil, at least. But that might cost you not less than Rupees Two. On your return, you can get her a cake of soap at least.'

When Ramnath left the house, Subhagyavati's body gave a shudder, as if struck by a knife. She had neither washed her hair, nor combed it. Her hair was dry for two days, it had ruffled. She thought that her husband should not have started the topic. 'I had kept it secret from Radha so far, but it was no secret now.'

Ramnath reached the bazaar. The child clung to his chest, turned his neck to the right and then to the left. The child was cheerful. 'I wish I could ask my father right now for all the things that I need!' The child thought.

'Papa, bread!' Stretching out the hand carrying the rupee coin, Krishna pointed to the nearby baker's shop that was filling the air with the pleasant smell of oven-fresh bread. Observing his father's silence, Krishna thought that if he insisted on having the very first thing that he saw, then all the other shops selling many other attractive things would be left out. His father would find an excuse for leaving all the shops.

A motorcar came from behind, and Ramnath started walking on the edge of the road. '*Poon.poon*. Papa, a *Poon.*

poon motor'" Then the child pointed towards a bicycle at a distance. 'That... there...there, *tanatana*..' The child drew his father's attention to the bicycle.

'I shall get you that too, but keep quiet.' His father said to him while walking onward. 'There is that tick-tick-tick...!' Kishna made him stop near a watchmaker's shop. He looked at the clock in the shop and knew that it was already 5 o'clock.

'Yes, this too we shall buy, but on our return. You better have *pakoras* first.' He tried to calm the child.

'Yeah...pakoras... ahaha... I shall not give any to Chama and Chenkala...! Chama beats me. Krishna is bad. I shall share the *pakoras* with my mother....' Kishna started insisting again. He was sure that it was only the *pakoras* that his father would fetch, and he might not fetch him other things.

Ramnath thought how many items could he purchase for Rupee One; which has devalued to a farthing now. And he longed to meet so many needs. 'He is insisting on the motor's *poon poon, tanatan* of the bicycle, and *tick tick* of the clock, and bread and *pakoras*. The child is very dangerous!' He thought.

On reaching near the bridge, Kishna made his father stop. He stopped for a while. He made him turn to a vendor sitting to the left. There was a broad wooden tray before the vendor that contained many grocery items; the attractive things had a shine that made Ramnath's eyes burn.

'Things like these are of no use to you.' He tried to make his son understand. 'But the bottle of oil... a cake of soap... and the mouth organ..! I wish the child took no notice of such things.' He looked into the eyes of the child and saw a stir in them. He was observing the disparate things one by one. He had the one-rupee coin with him, and was not supposed to leave without buying. He was yet to espy the mouth organ. In order to stop him from watching all, he took a turn, and the child remained silent, perhaps to favour his father, and the *pakora* vendor was yet to be visited.

Having walked a little further, he saw a bevy of people at the end of the street. A noise could be heard. Some people moved about restively and talked calmly. A couple of policemen were also present in the crowd. He could not understand what the matter was. He said to a passerby, 'Hey brother, what is the matter here?' But without saying anything in reply, the passerby walked away in a different direction, as if he had not heard him.

'Has there been a squabble?' He asked a few people who were busy talking to each other.

'HA-HAHA-HAHA! If it is not a squabble, what else would you call it? Do you think it is a dancers' spectacle?' One of the persons said to him in a scornful tone. Some other person was rather sympathetic to say, 'Oh Pundit, you might fall down with a shove of the little finger. You better save yourself and the child. What are you waiting for? A thief is a thief. He has committed some theft. He has stolen over Rupees Five hundred from somebody's pocket.'

'Rupees Five hundred! He has stolen; he is a

pickpocket!' He desired to see what a pickpocket actually looked like. He stood up on his toes to have a look. His surprise was uncontrollable.

When he actually saw that it was none other but Subhan barber's nephew who was caught by the police, his body felt the tremor of a current.

The child said, 'Papa, walk on, walk, *pakoras*!'

'No, not this way. There is no *pakora* seller in this street. Now keep quiet, or I shall not fetch you anything. Naughty child! Such things are of no use to you. Do not be crazy! I shall have to hold back this kind of attitude of yours. I shall destroy it. I do not want to get humiliated in my old age because of you. I do not want disgrace. I love my respect more than your life. Now my dear, please listen to me and let's go away.'

Taking long strides he walked and kept reflecting, 'Will Kishan Lal too become a pickpocket or a dacoit? No, never. I shall not let him become a dacoit. I had made a wrong assessment. Radha's son will not become a thief. But Kishan Lal might commit robbery in broad daylight and go behind bars. Radha's son shall get handcuffed. No, he should not commit any moral crime. I regret my wrong assessment. That was just my fancy, a wrong idea – hollow and baseless.'

He continued striding while the child was shedding torrents of tears. Since he was frightened by his father's meaningless talk, he did not even make a whimper or moaning. Perhaps he was inclined to narrate all this to his mother that his father did not fetch him even one thing out of that long list. He might return the rupee to his mother saying, 'Mother, please you get me *pakoras.*'

Ramnath espied the cinema advertisement that hung on the electric post at the brim of the road.

'Oh! Jeevan Lal and Madhu Sudhan. I shall surely let them enjoy a cinema show today at 5 o'clock.' He walked faster. Nearing his house, he looked around. The wayfarers noticed his restlessness. They wondered at his uneasiness.

He entered the narrow street and stopped at the door of his house. After looking around, he placed the child on the ground. His breathing was fast. He put his hand into the inner pocket of his coat. There were just Rupees Two there. But he needed one more rupee to support his plan. He cast a look at the child's hand; the one-rupee coin in his fist was wet with sweat. He clutched the child's hand.

'You are my good boy! You are really a nice boy. How good you are! Give me that one-rupee coin. I shall buy you a...'

He caressed the child's head with affection, but the child angrily released his hand from his father's hold.

'What! Oh no, never. I shall not let you become a thief. Give that rupee to me. You might drop it. It is not wise to keep a rupee in a child's hand.' Ramnath used his wit to persuade the child. Then he talked calmly to him, 'Give it to me. You were just a keeper. It was in your custody. Give it back to me!'

The two wrangled and bickered for a while to the best of their strength. Finally, he snatched the coin from his child's hand and fled. The child cried loudly while looking at his perspiring hand and entered his house with the intention of complaining about the father to his mother.

Fair and Black

The clock from Ramrakha Mal's house struck tan-tan-tan- seven. Shibram shook both his hands and with angry eyes watched a person who stood a distance away and then walked cowardly showing his back while uttering abuses.

'I wish I gave that possessed person a strong slap so that he remembered it for long. Tomorrow too, you bastard, I shall give you a thrashing at the same time, 7 o'clock, in the market, in the crowd of tourists!'

Roop Kishen heard the noise of the feud. The words 'at 7 o'clock' caused a stir in his body. He was shocked to the core of his heart, and his hand stopped writing. The sound tan-tan of the clock and Shibram's uttering '7 o'clock' increased his agitation. Shibram came near Ramrakha Mal's shop, and sat on the veranda. He moved his fingers through his hair, and to calm down his fervour of victory, breathed deep in the open.

Sitting inside, Roop Kishen moved the palm of his hand on his forehead with his head bowed down. His sentiments were disarrayed by his mental crisis. He did not concentrate on one issue, and was soon lost in some other chaos, and then was swayed by some third worry.

Whenever he thought of the tick-tick sound of the clock, he was overwhelmed by a similar mental agitation. His ears were habituated to hearing the same repetitive tick-tick-tick of the clock from opening his shop in the morning to eleven in the night, it was seldom that the sound scared him or that he was frightened. For instance, just a while ago Shibram had said 'tomorrow I shall beat you again, you bastard!' at this very hour, yes at '7 o'clock'. This made Roop Kishen morose. When someone from an affluent family, chose a golden wristwatch from the rows of watches at the showroom of the West End Watch Company and said, 'How much does it cost?' Roop Kishen was drowned in the world of forgetfulness.

Alas! The problem of the clock had become a source of doom, of anguish. Woman, clock and love! Ideas like this and her wrist... a world of evils, all these complexities... this inverted jar and roughness... my wrist is a little... I wonder what made that devil of a manager of the watch company think of my wrist. I love watches. What if the watch does not become my wrist? What shall happen if the watch stops its tick-tick while worn on my arm? What if I do not wind its spring daily to keep it moving? Or, if it does not what right do I have on this watch? I am sure that it shall not reveal the swarthiness of my wrist. It shall not let the roughness of my skin be revealed. Then I might try to remove the swarthiness of my scalp to look bright. Ah!

I curse my tummy, which made my white scalp become black in the scorching heat of India!

The manager of the West End Watch Company looked at Roop Kishen with scornful and sarcastic eyes. He wore a *Kamiz* and *Pyjamah* (shirt and trousers) made of cotton bought from the store of homemade things; he put a dull-coloured cap on his head. Roop Kishen was good looking by birth, but the blows of various misfortunes made him look haggard. Therefore, he said, 'I shall try to make my black scalp white again.'

On stepping in, he asked the manager of the watch company, 'Show me a wristwatch, please. What is the price of this one?'

In order to fathom his heart, the manager said just for fun, 'One hundred and fifty after discount.'

'Rupees One hundred and fifty!' Roop Kishen thought. 'I would gladly pay him even Rupees Two hundred. I do not like his offering me discount for finalising the deal at one shop only. I love this type of wristwatches. This watch, too, appears to be craving to be on my arm. What does this cruel manager mean by evincing a nonchalant smile?'

Having seen the wristwatch, he was almost convinced that it really longed to be worn on his arm. While lost in thoughts, Roop Kishen placed the watch back at its place in the cupboard.

Meanwhile the employees of the nearby shops assembled near Shibram. His laughter – 'hi-hi-hi' broke Roop Kishen's silence. He took out a cardamom from his pocket and put it into his mouth. He sensed much taunting in Shibram's laughter; his heart was jolted.

Shibram said to the bevy of employees, 'I might not be named Shibram if I do not make him cry for his mother's help!'

One of his audiences said rather confidentially, 'Now tell us what the matter is.' Some other person conjectured and said, 'It must be an issue in dealings. Baba, we have kept ourselves safe from the worries of dealings.'

Shibram was quick to add, 'That is how you keep life going. That idiot seems to be under some spell. I swear by Shri Rama that I shall exorcise this ghost from him. The 'lord' has fallen in love! He almost dies to eke Rupees Fifty, and still the lord is in love.'

Roop Kishen, sitting inside, sprang up, 'Love! Rupees Fifty! Oh! I just attained to earning Rupees Forty-five in the last month. Does it mean that I should never be in love? Then who the fortunate one is love meant for? Desire - longing - other words for the word love. Can't I then buy that wristwatch? I am just ready to pay more than Rupees One hundred and fifty. Doesn't that wristwatch too crave to be worn on my arm?'

Shibram continued saying, 'My daughter is now in her youth, I have to ready myself to get her married. The agreement has been almost finalised. But, *ha-ha-ha-* This tramp said that he was in love with her! I wonder what he could do to make her happy. He possesses hardly anything except those two or three dungeons of rooms filled with trash. One is used as a kitchen, and the other for a mattress, and the third filled with some cheap pictures. He has neither any ancestral belonging, nor anything of his own earning.'

Roop Kishen was now fed up with this tete-a-tate. He was after all incharge of the shop. He was both a clerk and an accountant. His account keeping was getting disturbed. Shibram's incensing words and sneers were like arrows that pierced his heart.

'Can't I afford to get the wristwatch cleansed? Shall I forget its maintenance? No.' While reflecting like that, he came out; his eyes were reddened with ire. He said, 'Shibram!'

Hearing him, the guys sitting near Shibram fell silent, and started staring at Roop Kishen.

'Shibram, I request you to stop talking. What is the fun of discussing such issues at the shop? Please get up now.' Then he hung his head.

He could not say anything more than that. He had been implored by Shibram sometime in the past: perhaps his father had borrowed Rupees Two thousand from Shibram on the occasion of his daughter's marriage and Roop Kishen had repaid that money in just two instalments after his father's death. Shibram could easily utter a few curses in his name, but musing about some secret, he could not utter anything. He was just a kid to him in comparison. And then he thought that if he gave a repartee to Roop Kishen's words 'leave now!' It was possible that Roop Kishen might not let him sit there from the next day where he had cried out 'The son of the *lord* is in love...' This was the reason that made Shibram sit silent. As soon as Roop Kishen entered, the persons sitting there started leaving.

An Indian young man and an English young girl, holding each other's arms, strolling over the *Bandh* walked that way. The young man was rather swarthy, and the English girl was snow-white. Her bare arms looked immaculate like milk, and softer than cream. Her body was bright white.

Roop Kishen saw them after turning towards that side. Two men sitting there came near him.

'Sir, walnut wood items! Wood carving! Papier-mâché - first class - Please visit *Rajab and Sons*.'

The other person said, 'Shawls! Pashmina! Fragrant saffron! Standard Company!'

The young Indian and his wife looked at each other and evinced a smile and walked ahead.

'How could they have met each other? This too is an issue to think about: An Indian young man and his spouse a European girl!' Roop Kishen could not make out how blackness dominated whiteness. He just wanted to get an explanation from Shibram. He always accepted defeat whenever he had a discussion with Shibram. This time, too, Shibram defeated Roop Kishen with his weak arguments; he could always sense that his fragile arguments soon broke like un-spun thread.

Roop Kishen called him calmly: 'Shibram!' The latter raised his head and looked at Roop Kishen who stood like a free cypress tree that was captivated by the love of the garden and the warble of the bulbul. Roop Kishen had made his scalp look black, but it was time that he somehow brightened it up, even if he had no option but to wipe it; he had felt the need now.

He opened the door and while entering, he said again, 'Shibram!'

Shibram was watching him intently till then. He replied smilingly, 'I get you, brother, I know what you want to say.' Having said this, he walked to Roop Kishen's room.

Seeing him rather worried, Shibram said to him, 'What has happened to you today? Why do you look so distressed? May I know why?'

The sound of the clock made Roop Kishen more restive. 'What worries me? Is it because the manager of the watch company had turned his head away when he cast a glance at his wrist?' He ruminated. 'The manager too is an Indian. What if his complexion is...'

The Sun had set. The employees of the shops at the Bandh sat and exchanged jokes and expressed their opinion on their respective way of working in the shops.

Roop Kishen feigned a smile and said to Shibram, 'There is one issue that needs to get resolved.'

'Say it, Sir. I am sure it must be a hollow problem. I am fed up of settling such problematic issues...'

Roop Kishen reflected on his naivety and told

Shibram all, even that the manager turned his head away on seeing his wrist.

Empathising with him, Shibram said, 'It is no trivial issue to go in for a wristwatch. And then this wrist of yours - Think. Just ponder over this.'

It was not a serious issue with Roop Kishen to go in for that costly wristwatch which he could not afford to buy. He had perceived that the watch of his choice was impatient to get worn on his wrist. 'If the heart of the watch was so fidgety for him, then was it not a hard stone in his spacious chest instead of a heart?' He continued musing again and again.

Shibram went away and Roop Kishen pondered more gravely on the black and white aspects of the world.

The next day when the horns of the cars on Residency Road parallel to the Bandh started sounding, white-skinned foreigners appeared on the roofs of the houseboats, adorned with lattices and the curtains, to enjoy the fresh breeze. Shibram was already squatting on the porch of Ramrakaha Mal's shop; chewing a cardamom. He settled the accounts with the houseboat man for the tents and sheds that were rented out to him for the night. Roop Kishen was occupied in reasoning the decrease in income of the shop that he had noticed for the past seven days.

In the meantime, Shibram masticating a cardamom, came in and sat in the chair that was near Roop Kishen's table. He said to him, 'Whenever I happen to see you, I find you troubled and morose and occupied in resolving delicate issues. Is all well?'

Roop Kishen raised his head and looked at Shibram. 'Oh! Forgive me please. Let me break some fresh news to you.'

Shibram had tried to fill the room with the sweet smell of the cardamom, yet Roop Kishen felt rather suffocated. Shibram took out another cardamom and tossing his tongue, gave it to Roop Kishen saying, 'Take it '

'Is it for something good?'

'Oh yes, one more thing, yesterday we finalised the marriage proposal of our daughter. You will have to make all arrangements. If anything is found wanting, you shall be held responsible. The bridegroom is Lala Kedarnath's son.'

In the meantime, Roop Kishen felt amazed that the tick-tick of the clock sounded dimmed. A gale of cold breeze blew in from the side of the Bandh, and exited through the window on the backside. The tick-tick sound fell silent.

'Oh!' Roop Kishen's eyes were wide open as he had forgotten to wind the clock. 'But, no, no.' He mused, 'I shall never forget to wind my wristwatch. Yes. I am sure. Never shall I forget. Oh, in case this comes to Shibram's mind, he shall certainly say laughingly with spoof that people like me are not worthy of buying a wristwatch. Only Lala Kedarnath and people of rank like him deserve it.'

His restlessness and agitation increased further and thus he asked Shibram, just to divert his attention, to go out for a while. He went in to wind the clock; the clock started ticking again.

There was one full week for making preparations for

the wedding of Shibram's daughter. Roop Kishen visited the showroom of West End Watch Company twice in two days. Before entering the showroom, he assessed the demeanour of the manager. This made him drift miles away from his decision.

'If the manager contorts his brows on seeing my hair dye... If he turns his neck away from me... Oh! What shall I do then?'

Twice he returned back in disappointment. And then, one night when the wedding party was scheduled to arrive in the morning, Roop Kishen restlessly paced the veranda of his house; he was most disturbed that day. He perceived the tick-tick sound as heavier than the strike of a hammer. He was musing on the significance of a wristwatch; he concluded that his life was incomplete without it. He got up and entered the backyard of his house. It was quite windy. Dense clouds had overcast the sky. There too his restiveness was not assuaged. He turned back, but he had hardly come to his earlier position when he heard a sound, although quite dim, in the wind. 'Go, go!'

He stood flabbergasted, with widened eyes. He could not perceive anything in the dark. He stopped walking and listened intently, 'Go, my Pran Nath, go. Don't you forget me. I swear by your feet. You dwell in every iota of my being. But... but ...'

'Please do not weep. Do not be so cowardly. I do not expect this from you. Love is another name for empathy. Both of us possess empathy for each other, and it shall always be there. And now understand that this made us achieve whatever we wanted. I am leaving!' Tears welled up in Roop Kishen's eyes. He quickened his pace towards his house.

'Was he the one who was told by Shibram with the intention of thrashing him, "I shall beat him tomorrow at this very spot." The *brother of my wife* (slang) is in love! He has just three rooms! He gets just Rupees Fifty as monthly salary from Atmaram Brothers. But why did he refuse something that he was about to get? Is it his cowardice or what?' Lost in such musings, he was home.

The next morning he had forgotten Shibram and the noise near his house, he intensely wished for the wristwatch. Before going to his own shop, he went to the showroom of West End Watch Company. The new manager was yet to arrive. An employee of the company recognised him and said, 'Come in, Roop Kishenji!'

'Please get the wristwatch of that day.'

'Wristwatch! Oh! I sold it just now... just now. Lala Kedarnath's son, you know, is getting married.'

He felt as if he had lost the energy to keep standing. His head grew heavier and hung down. He rested his back against the wall. He had completely given in. But Shibram's brother-in-law had said to his beloved before departure: 'Don't you be cowardly ...'

He mustered courage and said, 'How much did you sell it for?'

The employee laughed in such a way as if he wanted to convey to Roop Kishen that he was experienced, and that he had learnt early in his career the knack of shopkeeping and being humble to customers. He said to him, 'For Rupees Fifty. He had a catch almost for free.'

Roop Kishen left while looking repeatedly at his own wrist. 'It is yet to get whiter. It was yet to be rubbed - I might try to rub it now. Perhaps, now…! '

Acquiescence

I did not know anything about where we were going, but my companion knew. He was fully familiar with footprints, depths and heights of the labyrinthine paths. What I barely knew was that Babuji had called me to his village where his headquarter was. In terms of kinship, Babuji was my brother who worked in the Social Welfare Department as the Overseer.

The name of my companion was probably Khaliq - yes Khaliq Khan who possessed a fragile frame with plenty of wrinkles on his forehead. His beard was of a hand's length. He spit time and again and because of the chill the moisture froze on the hair of his beard. A home-made garment of thick cloth covered his body. His trousers were made of a woollen fabric that was wrapped up in woollen putties. His entire possession was a horse that I rode, and he strode ahead holding the bridles.

Being winter, it was rather harshly chilly that day. Black and thick clouds were drifting in the sky. We two moved on the bridle-path that meandered through the rice fields. I was amazed to see the twists and turns in the path. Being seated for six long hours on the saddle, I felt my whole body was wearied to exhaustion. I started ruminating: 'This fragile and thin man has been saying since morning "the village is just behind the next field, yes, that copse of willows...We are just about to reach there." I am deadly tired, and he does not even mention his fatigue.'

I said to Khaliq, 'My Master, how far is it now? Are these serpentine meandering paths ever going to end anywhere?'

'Just in a while,' Kaliq said calmly while continuing at his pace. 'A couple of more fields and you will be at Babuji's house.'

Babuji always called him Metha because he was the leader of the group of all the coolies who worked under his command. He was fully acquainted with the twists and turns of all the paths and roads, whether metalled or un-metalled. His entire life, this was his sole vocation. After God, he had unfailing trust only in Babuji.

Time and again, I looked at him and pondered over his naivety. After a brief silence, I said to him, 'Khaliq, will you come with me to the city?'

'No Sir.' Khaliq said in a scornful tone. 'Only my foes might go to the city. We never borrow money from any lender. Why should I go to the city? And then you might be knowing the proverb that *a sparrow belongs in the forest.*'

I could understand nothing of his logic. He lived just twenty-two miles away from the city, yet he perhaps believed that the city is visited only by those people who are following cases of criminal charges which could not be settled by the Committee of Elders of the village. There were only a few guys in his village who left their work, and walked for four to five days to reach the city, I kept mum.

'Do you get me or not?' Khaliq completed his sentence after some pause. 'Only such persons go there who borrow or lend money but keep the accounts murky. Have we ever kept even a paisa unpaid? I repaid even the debt of my late grandfather now in paradise.'

'You are no poor man, I think,' I said to him. 'Only such a person could be considered poor who has no land of his own or has no job to do, and as such is not able to afford food; one who is helpless. And Kaliq you …'

He was surprised. After having a short rest, he said, 'Land? I did not get any. Those who were destined to get, got it.' Consoling himself, he said further, 'No Sir, I am not poor. How does it matter that I did not get a piece of land? All is true. Yet I have trust in God; I believe in destiny.'

His manners, behaviour, and dress revealed that if there is any such form or shape made by God as proves through dress and manner of conversing, that it is good to have unfailing faith and acquiescence that is Khaliq.

I inquired further, 'Do all the people living in your village have trust in God or have faith in Him?'

Khaliq said promptly and with an air of pride, 'There are many who have faith, but there are some who do not. Yes Sir, those who have no faith in God deserve hell. Yes, of late there has been a trend that many people do not rely on what God bestows upon them.'

I responded with an expressionless smile. I espied his dirty and murky chest that was covered with ruffled grey hair, and was naked as a cliff. Yet he wore a red turban on his head that had an aura of pride about it. The turban proved that the coolies under his subordination respected him. Besides, the turban also evidenced that he would be commanding respect in his entire village.

After a short while I said again, 'Khaliq, now you are an elderly person. Don't you feel any fatigue?'

'We know no fatigue.' He said with laughter. 'Our skin is quite thick. Our attire, too, is thick. And, because of Babuji, we enjoy a comfortable life.'

The area under Babuji was spread over about thirty square miles. Khaliq's job was to supervise the work of the coolies. In addition to this routine job, he helped Babuji with his duty. In spite of all this, Babuji had a sort of scorn for him. After much insistence he would say, 'Who?..That cadaver Khaliq? He is very sluggish. He is spoiled by our undue care for him.' We are familiar with such habitual words from Babuji. He was wont to utter one or the other slang whenever there was mention of Khaliq. This bewildered me.

'Do you always stay in rest? Do they not make you work?' I asked Khaliq.

He stopped the horse. Casting an angry look at me, he said, 'Sir, you are being funny, perhaps. If I do not work, what shall I get to feed myself? Who is there to bear my whims, that too in our times?'

With the intention of having fun, I said to him, 'You know, you have always been parsimonious. Is it good to have temptation in old age? After completing your duty of overseeing, you shall leave the world. The doors of paradise shall be flung open for you to enter. Thus, you shall get rid of your needs'

He seemed to find in my words what he had searched for in his entire life. I sensed brightness in his eyes. He heaved a sigh of relief. With a sense of joy all the pleasures and tranquillity of paradise surged in his eyes. He said as soon as I finished my words. 'Sir, what you said is to the point. I told you that faith is a big trial from God Almighty. His abode is infinitely spacious. All those in need extend their hands to Him. There is no question of disappointment. But those who withstand all moments of trust and patience without a grudge are sure to enjoy the pleasures of paradise. Ah-ha-ha! Sir! Paradise! How do I explain it to you?'

I reflected inwardly that our country is in no way inferior to paradise. We have golden fields, springs of icy water, and never-withering verdant forests!

I was again a little tardy to move ahead. He held the bridle with both hands behind him. I espied a distant plane tree that was in our path. I noticed something strange that invited my attention. I asked Khaliq to look towards that spot and then said, 'Khaliq, I feel rather fatigued now. Let us rest for some time under the tree there. I think I shall not be able to continue moving further. I feel my entire body is aching. You are quite well and robust to walk, much like a young man.'

There was a spring under the plane tree. The very sight of the spring made me feel a burning thirst. I took a couple of handfuls of water to quench my thirst. I heaved a long breath to relax and sat beside Khaliq. I bloated a little, and said, 'My Overseer, the water of the spring is very sweet. You might not find this type of water even in paradise!'

Khaliq said in reply, 'Sir, it is Babuji's graciousness that the walls of spring were made concrete last year.' Having said this, he gave a deep sigh, hid his head between his two legs. I knew it already that Khaliq was thin and weak. Being wearied, he bowed down his head.

The chilling wind coming from all the four sides almost benumbed my face and ears. The sky was overcast with clouds, as I had noticed at the time of setting out. Birds were seen sitting in the humpy and trimmed trees, or flying away from them.

I stood up and started to stroll a little. I looked far and near. A bridle-path could be seen running through the nearby fields. A long row of poplar trees was visible only two or three hundred yards away. Just near the plane-tree there was a shanty made of unbaked bricks. The locale increased my interest; a simmering agitation was in my heart. My eyes widened and I was in a frenzy-like condition. Having watched all aspects of the ambience, I walked back towards Khaliq, and was reminded of something. I said to him, 'Khaliq, do you notice that long row of poplars there?'

Khaliq raised his head and said, 'Yes Sir. It is the National Highway, General Road!'

I was amazed, and cast a glance at the shanty again. The agitation in my mind intensified.

'When was this spring made concrete?' I asked Khaliq.

He gave me a reply while keeping his head bowed down. 'Only last year, Sir.'

I was further surprised by all the four replies given by Khaliq as they confirmed my idea that I had chanced to see that place earlier as well. I stood up again and after taking a few steps, I returned to Khaliq again. There were tears in my eyes, and I said to him restively, 'Khaliq!'

He gave me no reply, but only 'Oh!' came out from his mouth without his control. I saw a queer shine in his eyes that conveyed despondence. I could not understand anything about Khaliq's this strange behaviour; I was almost terrified. I asked him again, 'What has happened to you, Khaliq?'

He raised his head and looked towards me; big drops of tears welled up in his eyes. The tears dropped and made his beard wet and glistened. 'What made you ejaculate "Oh?" Did you remember something?'

With tears running down his cheeks, Khaliq said, 'I was just praying for the dead. But what! Your eyes too are filled with tears? Why?'

Before asking him whose soul was he praying for, I said with the intention of diverting his attention. 'Nothing. I was feeling a sort of tumult in my heart.'

'Tell me what made you cry? What made you shed tears?'

While wiping his tears, Khaliq said, 'I prayed for the soul of Jani. She passed away last year. What a woman Jani was!'

He again wiped tears from his eyes and said, 'Jani was my wife. Before breathing her last, she had told me that she desired a place like this one where her body could be interred. She always considered spots like this as paradise. I loved her very much and she always kept me happy. But what could I do other than have firm faith in Him who took her away from me.'

In order to console Khaliq, I said, 'Khaliq, you better get out of this thought. Do not house such ideas in your heart, or you might become mad. That is what we call patience and perseverance. Have faith.'

While consoling him, tears dropped from my eyes. He felt as if I showed empathy for him and thus do him some favour, but my idea was …

We started our journey again. He said while clearing tears from his eyes, 'My wife has passed away, and you weep for nothing.'

Stopping, I said to him, 'Not for nothing do I weep.

Only the one knows the pang who has received to strike at the heart, Khaliq. I too am weeping over my destiny.'

Hearing my words, he stood still like a statue and stared at me. After a little thought, he said, 'What do you mean by that?'

'Khaliq, it is a matter that is beyond the ken of your mind - I was once in love, and my love too was lost in dust at the same place. Yes, I remember quite vividly, exactly at the same spot. But now she is no more, nothing is left behind. It was like a fire that doused before it flared out and was reduced to ashes. Yes, Khaliq, one day she, in company with her kin, had come to attend a wedding feast. We too were there. On our way back to the city, our boat stayed in the river athwart the metalled road; it stayed over two hours. They too stopped there. They were out of the boat on a random walk, and I too, was walking over that bridle path - that begins from the row of the poplar trees, and reached there... Khaliq, better walk faster as it is about to become dark... Then on seeing this spring, and feeling the environment I forgot everything, even my own self. After a while, she too chanced to reach there. When she found me lost in musings, she asked me what I was musing about. Getting no reply from me, she said, 'Are you to compose poetry? Crazy fellow!' I kept hearing her words... Khaliq, I hope you got me now. I think she expressed her first feelings of love for me. She went up to the spring, got cold water in her two hands put together, and splattered it on my face. My God, I was all flabbergasted to see her courage. She did not know that

I was already having feelings of love for her, but had not expressed them to her. But when I noticed her undaunted behaviour, I was completely nonplussed. She kept staring at me for a pretty long while. Then she looked around. I observed desire and hope in her eyes. There was rapture in her way of laughing that intimated to me that nature had a message of love… She looked at me a second time and said, 'What are you thinking about? Are you still under the spell? Are you still mad? Khaliq, are you being bored by such words of mine? I took you out from your pious feelings and made you hear my love story!'

'So, after that, my lips started fluttering and a wild joy danced in my mind. I looked deep into her eyes, and said calmly to her, "I was in fact in search of you. You are the one who is my madness… Come, come closer, Oh my soul!" I saw glistening tears of love in her eyes. I approached her and took her in an embrace. I kissed her in the intensity of my passion… This was the beginning of my love that reached its climax, then and there. The world deemed it better to keep her at a distance from me. What could I do, Khaliq, for I was helpless? Our love did not consummate into marriage. I remember nothing about her other than the intense heat of love… And nothing beyond that.'

Khaliq stopped his paces and said to me, 'Yes Sir, look at me. What could I do? I suggest you too rely on your destiny. Acquiesce in your destiny. What else can you do?'

Khaliq's reply made me feel the ground under my

feet slid. I did not feel any satire in his words, but a hard slap that shall leave its imprints on me forever.

I was remorseful at those words that I spoke to him before reaching the spot of the spring. There was no fathoming my repentance. I said calmly to him, 'It is okay, Khaliq. I could do nothing. I could not find any remedy to the ailment …'

I felt that the heat that made me writhe in pain might turn into tuberculosis to make me rot from within.

Babuji's house was just in view, I saw him at his window smiling to see us there.

The Surge

It was midnight when she woke up all of a sudden, and got up. Sitting on the bed, she fumbled around to find the lamp, turned it up, and lit it. Then she rubbed her half-open eyes with her fingers. After looking to her left with her heavy eyes, she heaved a long and cold sigh. An uncontrolled 'Ah!' came out from her mouth. 'The world of dreams is really full of light,' she reflected, 'Once you open your eyes you find gloomy darkness all around you.'

She had woken up from her dream; the sweet but half-finished dream made her morose. Looking around herself with her sad eyes, she found something wanting. Was it the dream of love that had betrayed her? Who were her eyes seeking in that room?

Thus, she shivered after having some hazy dream. She assessed every organ of her body.

Oh! Who knows why she hid her face with her two

hands? She had been lying and changing sides on her bed for the whole day after getting exhausted with fatigue. Now her sleep was disrupted, she continued sitting on her bed.

A wedding procession had entered the village only a few days ago. She thought of her friend Noori who had left for her in-laws house after saying adieu to her parents. She could still feel the echoes of the reed-pipes and drums in the air. She remembered the bright light of the torches, women's lamenting-like wedding songs, and their following the palanquin. She recollected how she secretly managed to see her friend Noori in the palanquin and how she shed tears. All this was vividly dancing before her eyes. Then in the dim light of the oil-lamp, many reminiscences brought tears to her eyes. She felt like a stray bitch whose cubs are taken away from her and she roams the streets in their search. She consoled herself by weeping the whole day, but felt the urge to weep again. And then she crooned a song. Who had taught her the song? The song was always sung by Na'eem, the son of the land-surveyor. Could she not sing any other song? There were many other popular songs that were sung in the village.

She felt that the past couple of months of her life were as long as four hundred years. The last time he had come to take her leave, she was having a very nice time. She had said to Rasool, 'I shall keep you posted on my sister's address.' 'It might be that he later forgot what he had promised. Men are quick in forgetting... but ... no, no… Last month he had sent a parcel containing cloth for my trousers and dry dates covered with glue paper from across the sea on Rahim Chacha's address. Besides, he had written that he was going even farther from where he was… *Hanh!* Does it mean that he forgot me?'

'I wish he was dismissed from his service! Who knows what job? Oh, I wish… what shall I do?'

After thinking and musing she looked at her eyes, the bulge of her chest, and every organ of her body. Then she again felt a shiver running through her body. It was some invisible fear that caused it, just like the idea of a snake makes a snake-bitten person feel it. She again lay down on her bed to take restless turns… The silence in the house was broken by the bleating of an ewe. 'I am no better than this mute animal,' she thought. 'Who is there to fathom my heart's closet and hear my grief? Who is there to listen to me?'

My father and mother got scared of my prime youth and were anxious to get me engaged to someone. Yet she was lost in the world of her dreams. 'If he does not turn up… but he had assured me that he would be back by the end of the rainy season when I would be busy reaping in the field… And Na'eem too had given me a promise like that! But next Friday we shall go to the fields with our sickles. When will he return? When… He had also said that he would engage Lala and the village chief to discuss about her marriage. *Hunhh!* He doesn't have guts … but I too am not ready to get married. My mother and father love me a lot, they really need me. I am their darling daughter. Oh! When is he to return? He knows it well that after harvesting is finished and there are moonlit nights ... when the villages reverberate with the sounds of reed-pipes ...marriages take place... what should I do?'

How deep was her anxiety? How despondent was she? This was a problem to which she wanted Na'eem to come up with the solution. He was the one whom she could ask. She again looked around and then shut the window. There was someone nearby who looked at her with desire...she opened the window again and then shut it. 'Oh! These dark trees too ogle at me and harass me by watching my movements!' She moved her hand softly over her bulging breasts... The very touch of her fingers awakened her senses just as a languid snake is awakened. She wanted the other, and tears surged again in her eyes, and then she wept. In the meantime, the day dawned.

In the morning while she was busy picking leaves of collard from her kitchen garden, she heard laughter from the other bed of the vegetable field. She shrunk with fear. 'Who is there to interrupt the silence?' She espied the son of her paternal aunt Jamal, standing near the fence of the vegetable field. She busied herself in her work; no word came out from her mouth. In her despondence she mused, 'Let the cursed fellow know that after all he was her own cousin.'

'Hi-hi-hi...' Seeing her, Jamal gave another giggle. It appeared that he knew nothing more than that kind of laughter! He intimated his ideas only through laughter! This laughter, clumsy and awkward, he used without any sense of time. This was perhaps the beginning as well as the end of his knowledge. 'Is it that all the joys of his life are concealed in that one laughter? What! Is it that this laughter is his guide to the new path and towards Zooni?' She mused further, 'If my mother and Lala try their utmost, I will not accept. I will never give in even if Jamal strives hard, holds my chin in imploring, even then I will not agree.' While musing like that she had already come out of the first bed of collard and was busy in the second. Her hand moved faster than the scissors.

She tidily collected the collard leaves in her right hand. Perhaps it was her habit to gather collard leaves every morning, and perhaps she would continue doing so. The dew drops on the collard leaves shone. With the touch of her hand the dew drops, like mercury, became restive, fell and got absorbed in the soil. She thought that her heart was more fragile than the dew drops. 'Even the touch of my hand makes them quiver! Most of the times my restiveness increases a thousand times more than the stirred dew drops!'

Jamal was still standing against the fence and gazing at her. The red lines of the embroidery on his white cap were visible even from a distance. The cap looked glued to his shaven skull. He wore a shirt made of raw cotton that had dropped all the buttons, and thus, his chest was bare. The chest looked like a bared cliff, but rather wider. His face was chubby. Zoon was the life of his hopes.

He took out a small box from the pocket of his shirt. Took a pinch of snuff and rubbed it on his teeth. After a little while, he closed his mouth, and with a fixed gaze at the bend of Zooni's back, he kept smiling. Her newly sewed black garment and white-dotted trousers increased Jamal's restlessness. Black coloured head-cover and black tuft of hair braids dangled from her right arm to her left arm. Time and again she stopped to tidy her braids. Seeing her tidying her tresses, Jamal placed his hand over his chest and heaved a long sigh. He could hear the jingle of her bangles and the sweet but low tinkle of her dangling silver ear-pendants. Jamal mused, 'Oh, hopefully they would finish the cropping earlier! Today, I shall move the sickle faster, and leave all others behind so they are wiser. Then I shall call Zeendar Baba who shall whole-heartedly bestow a sack of paddy on me. I shall invite the entire village for a feast. And Zoon!... she shall be in the palanquin amidst the oil-torches. The palanquin bearers… Gafoor, Kabir Khan, Ramzan… shall not waste even a moment to change their shoulder support.'

Having thought to that extent, Jamal could still not muster enough courage to utter even a word when he was near Zoon.

He laughed a third time, and then said, 'Zoon, is Lala at home?'

Hearing this, Zoon stretched herself like a cypress tree. Being angry, she said, 'Why are you gnawing at my brain? My grass-shoes might talk to you. *Hunh*!'

Jamal left, gibbering something to himself.

She sat on the ridge and started musing again, 'In

case Na'eem does not turn up, what should I do? What shall be my fate if I am wedded off to this tramp? Oh!... why did I give a pat reply to Jamal?... What will he do in front of my father and mother? What shall be Jamal's reaction to me? And what next?... No, no... That can never happen!... Na'eem has to come back.'

Her father's image appeared before her eyes. Then she felt some unknown shivering, she got terrified. She thought of her friend who was to visit her father's house and will say to her without a pause, 'Zooni, I wish you too got wedded off!' Then I shall have a lot of tete-a-tate with her. But her shy talk shall increase my restlessness and nothing more than that... Na'eem shall return. I wish he would come today itself!' ... Lost in such musings, she silently reached the compound of her house. A thin smoke was coming out from one of the windows and getting dispersed in the dry air of the morning. The door of the barn underneath the stairs of the house was open and the nasty smell of cattle urine emanated from it. The cattle bawled for hay and oil-cakes, perhaps waiting for Zoon to come. She kept her basket containing the collards aside and entered the barn to provide oil-cakes to the cattle.

While spreading hay in the manger, she heard her father speaking. He said, 'Saifullah flatly refused, he does not possess even a penny.' Zoon's mother said in reply, 'Dishonest person ignoring his word. Only day before yesterday he said that we could borrow from him as easily as water. Zoon belongs to them as she belongs to me... '

'Does it mean that...'

'Would he lend us in God's name? Why? Who has ever asked him for money without interest? He would not die if he lends us money against mortgage.'

'He told me that all the milkmen of the area took all his money against butter otherwise he had waited only for us.'

'What did Gaffar Khan say?'

Her husband evinced a ray of hope on his face and said to her, 'He shall lend us money, if God wishes.'

'Are we to mortgage our property and cattle?'

'Yes, he shall provide them with daily feed. He might say that they have not finished reaping the crop, and all are busy. I am yet to get money from anywhere.'

'Then he should tell the poor fellows how long to wait.'

A mixed feeling of despondence and joy appeared on Zoon's face. 'I wish Na'eem would come till then!'

When her father came outdoors, she came out of the barn, droning something to herself.

This was her usual morning. In the evening some boisterous laughter could be heard at the bank of the stream. Three women sat there with their feet in water. The woman sitting between the other two was given a nudge; the two repeatedly put their bodies on her or made her lie down on the grass. They also took their mouths close to her ears to whisper something to her. The woman sitting in the centre wore an embroidered head-cover. The hem of her *Pheran* (a loose outer garment) was also embroidered. Her trouser was made of double threaded dotted cotton. When Zoon saw her from a distance, she almost went running to her. The woman too, saw her coming towards her. All the three women took out their feet from the water, and the middle one hastened to stand up and held Zoon in a hug.

'Are you well, Zoon? What have you done to your eyes? These red lines … '

'Nothing. There was smoke coming out from the earthen oven that is why my eyes are teary. You tell me something about yourself. You put kohl in your eyes yourself, or asked someone to do it? Your face is blushing... Are you so engrossed in the joys of your life that you forgot us?'

'If Allah wills it, you too shall get married soon … I shall tell you after that what it is. Does your mouth water?'

Zoon wished to share all her secrets with her. The doused fire in her bosom flared up slowly. Having seen Noor, her eyes in search of something, tried to find it in Noor's eyes. Having seen Noor's blooming and bright face, she discovered what she wanted to find out. Even Noor could know it. Zoon stood with her head bowed; tears flowed from her downcast eyes.

Seeing her shedding silent tears, Noor said to her, 'I shall tell my mother that Zoon spends her days in weeping.'

Zoon had no reply.

Another woman said to her, 'Why do you hide your

woe from us? These tears surge from your heart. Noor, my sister! If they still delay your marriage that shall not be good for you. Hajra and Jana also got married; only one girl is left and that is Zoon. Let's ask Lala to get you married to Jamal ... '

The third woman interrupted, 'Neither you nor I can express what pleasures there are in married life - I was married last year, but the elation remains unabated even now!'

The second woman said abruptly, 'Why? Why can't we express it? You talk just of your own, when only a year has elapsed since your marriage, while in my case, two years have glided by, and even when I have a son Aziz in my lap. And Ismail might be now almost one year old. In spite of all that, I can never forget those pleasures that I had after marriage. Zoon, marriage must take place when you are in your prime.'

Zoon, heavy with perturbation, sat with her head bowed. The terse remarks by the three women caused a tumult in her mind. Noor and her other friends were already married. Even Hajra and Jana enjoyed their conjugal life. The slumbering serpent in Zoon's heart woke up again. While keeping her head down, she assessed every organ of her body. An unknown fear made her quiver.

She thought, 'If Na'eem does not turn up, let it be Jamal ... Ah! Perhaps, Na'eem will not return. May be he has forgotten me ...But he had given me a promise that he would return in the harvesting season and settle everything ... He even sent me a parcel ... He is sure to return ... But when? I wish he had come by now! Even if he returns, would he be able to tell my father that he has a desire for me? And then Lala has not behaved well with the Land-Surveyor! He is not to turn up, perhaps ... let him not come ...' She wiped her tears. Being swayed by the tide of emotions, she felt stirred. But that kind of stirring she had experienced several times in her jinxed body. Many times it even made her pull her hair. She decided to forget everything. She raised her head and looked at Noor. 'Lala has already decided about my marriage,' she said to Noor, 'only the opportune time is awaited.'

Noor said to Zoon, 'Do not hide to share the great fun you experience after getting married. But you have never hidden anything from me so far, why should you now? And in case you do not have fun, tell me. I shall be held accountable. But I am not telling you any lie. And such things are hardly expressed in words.'

In the meantime, the entire atmosphere was overwhelmed by grimness. Athwart the small stream, there flowed a canyon along the hem of the mountain. It was the force and indifferent flow that showed its course. It appeared that this time it might change its course again. Who knows how many things might get swept away in its spate... But Noor's expression intimated much to Zoon.

Ten days after that meeting, Zoon got married. She was amazed. There was neither any blush nor redness on her cheeks. She could not make it to meet Noor even when many days elapsed after her marriage. Her restiveness and desire increased day after day. Perhaps, she was not contented. The quiver that used to shake her and even devastate her before her marriage re-emerged. She used to cry and then laugh. Her angered face showed that she wanted to pull out Noor's hair. She felt her cheeks had sunk. Her complexion was becoming swarthy. All the new clothes, new trousers, for which Na'eem had sent her the cloth, and also the kohl for her eyes, all appeared useless. She thought that Na'eem did not turn up. 'If he comes, he has to answer my questions. But now it was an altogether different situation. Noor's guarantee is sufficient.'

After a few days of restiveness, she returned to her parental house. She met Noor at the appointed spot. She wished to devour her whole and strangle her friend so she could not even scream. No sooner did she meet Noor, than she asked her about the cause of her anxiety and woe, but there was no reply. Zoon's nostrils quivered with anger and blood surged in her veins. A torrent of tears came out from her eyes.

'You ruined me Noor!' Zoon burst out. 'You strangled me … I did not have any feeling of joy after getting married. I was better as I was. Why did you do so? Didn't you have pity on me?' The banks of the canyon caved in.

Noor, completely nonplussed, could not think or say anything. She burst into tears and held Zoon in a tight embrace. 'Why didn't you feel the joy? Oh! What do you say?' Then she whispered in her ear.

'No, no, Noori. That … *that* did not give me any joy. It was not a new thing for me. What did you do to me? You left me unable to face the world?'

Noor, still amazed, said, 'What! It was not a new thing to you? What does it mean?'

'Yes, I say it was not new to me. If you trust me, look! Oh my Na'eem! What shall I do now?'

The banks were adrift. The river had swayed many things. Zoon, with her head bowed, pointed to the protuberance of her belly.

Weighed by anxiety and worries she swooned and fell to the ground.

Som Nath Zutshi

Career Milestones

- By age 13, he had read some of the world-famous writers including *Karl Marx*, *Nikolai Gogol*, *Henry Ibsen* and *Franz Kafka*.
- At the age of 15 he had started writing short stories in Urdu language.
- At 19, he became the founding member of the *Quomi Cultural Front* which later became *Progressive Writers Front.*
- He began to write in Kashmiri language in 1947 when he turned 24.
- In 1948, he was just 25, Som Nath he took over as secretary of the *Progressive Writers Association,* and continued till 1954.
- In 1948, he wrote the first ever short story in Kashmiri language *Yeli Phol Gaash (When it was*

dawn) that was translated into many Indian as well as foreign languages, as were his other stories later.

- At the age of 28, he became the editor of Kashmir's first ever literary magazine *Kong Posh (Saffron Flower)* - from 1951 to 58.
- For his deep insight into the Kashmiri literature, he was made a member of the Reviewing Committee of the J&K Sahitya Academi.
- His dramas and stories were published in leading Indian media because of the beauty and depth of their content.
- He was the recipient of a number of awards and accolades for his works, including, among others, the coveted *Sahitya Akademi* award for creative writing, *Soviet Land Nehru* award for translating Gogol's *Inspector General* and from *All India Radio* for several radio plays telecast nationally in several languages including *Tae Whyeth Rooz Pakaan (And Jhelum Flowed).*
- He retired as Secretary to the Govt of J&K.
- He was invited from time to time, to be a member of the Selection Committee and Judging Committee, by the J&K Academy of Art, Culture and Languages, for appointments and to review the literary works of writers etc.